Praise for Heather MacAllister

"Witty, romantic, sexy and fun."
—*New York Times* bestselling author Christina Dodd

"Curling up with a Heather MacAllister romance is
one of my favorite indulgences."
—*New York Times* bestselling author
Debbie Macomber

"A one-sitting read for me. I got so caught up
in this story that I really didn't want it to end."
—*The Best Reviews* on *Male Call*

"The plot was inspired, the dialogue was witty and
the secondary characters were extraordinary."
—*Writers Unlimited* on
How To Be the Perfect Girlfriend

"Pure fantasy in the finest sense,
Heather MacAllister's *Never Say Never*
crackles with sexy banter."
—*Romantic Times BOOKreviews*

"Funny, fabulous, fantastic! Heather MacAllister
is at the top of my must-read list."
—*USA TODAY* bestselling author
Barbara Dawson Smith

"Smart, witty and fun...no one does it better than
Heather MacAllister."
—Award-winning author Amanda Stevens

Blaze

Dear Reader,

My sister got married last year and, as her matron of honor, I happily immersed myself in all things wedding, including the hunt for the perfect dress. And I learned a very important thing: fitting-room curtains and flimsy doors are not soundproof.

As I waited in changing rooms and salon viewing areas, I overheard brides talking about everything. By everything, I mean the groom and sex. The more time brides spent trying on wedding dresses, the more indiscreet they became. Then I wondered if the grooms were talking, too. And what would happen if the bride and groom overheard each other.

The result is my first book for Harlequin Blaze, *Undressed*. I hope you enjoy these four stories, which explore what *could* possibly happen when you've have four talkative couples—and a *very* thin wall between the fitting rooms of a bridal salon and the tuxedo rental store next door.

I'd love to know what you think of my first Blazing endeavor. If you'd like to learn more about *Undressed*, you can visit me at www.HeatherMacAllister.com.

Best wishes,

Heather MacAllister

Heather MacAllister

UNDRESSED

HARLEQUIN®

TORONTO • NEW YORK • LONDON
AMSTERDAM • PARIS • SYDNEY • HAMBURG
STOCKHOLM • ATHENS • TOKYO • MILAN • MADRID
PRAGUE • WARSAW • BUDAPEST • AUCKLAND

Recycling programs
for this product may
not exist in your area.

ISBN-13: 978-0-373-79477-5

UNDRESSED

Copyright © 2009 by Heather W. MacAllister.

ABOUT THE AUTHOR

Heather MacAllister lives near the Texas gulf coast where, in spite of the ten-month growing season and plenty of humidity, she can't grow plants. She's a former music teacher who married her high school sweetheart on the Fourth of July, so is it any surprise that their two sons turned out to be a couple of firecrackers? Heather has written more than forty romantic comedies, which have been translated into twenty-six languages and published in dozens of countries. She's won a Romance Writers of America Golden Heart Award, *Romantic Times BOOKreviews* awards for best Harlequin Romance and best Harlequin Temptation, and is a three-time RITA® Award finalist. When she's not writing stories, Heather collects vintage costume jewelry, loves fireworks displays, computers that behave and sons who answer their mother's e-mail. You can visit her at www.HeatherMacAllister.com.

Books by Heather MacAllister
HARLEQUIN TEMPTATION
981—CAN'T BUY ME LOVE
1014—FALLING FOR YOU
1025—NEVER SAY NEVER

To Pam Menz Baker and the XromX Pursuit group

Prologue

AT 9:20 P.M. on a Tuesday night, after trying on forty-three wedding dresses over three bridal-salon appointments during which her entourage of eight consumed several bottles of domestic sparkling wine, Cara Brantley at last found her perfect wedding gown.

Beth Ann Grakowski, aka Elizabeth Gray of Elizabeth Gray Bridal Salon in Rocky Falls, Texas, lived for such moments. The look of a dream matching reality…followed by the sentimental tears…the happy smiles…the hugs…the healthy profit when a designer gown sold…she loved it all. Someday, it would be *her* dream matching reality, *her* sentimental tears, *her* happy smile, *her* fantasy wedding financed by years of hard work… but until then, by golly she was going to make sure as many Texas brides got their happily-ever-after storybook wedding dress as she could.

On the way to her office to get the paperwork started, Beth snagged a leftover bottle of champagne for a private, self-congratulatory toast.

"Nooooo!" A wail echoed through the salon.

Beth Ann froze. Her clients were having a happy moment, *the* happy moment. There should be no wailing during happy moments.

"How could that have happened?" Mrs. Brantley's voice rose.

Beth nearly dropped the credit card that would let Cara Brantley walk down the aisle in a strapless, crystal-encrusted mermaid gown designed by Georgia Hanover.

"It's ruined!" sounded clearly through the wall Beth's office shared with the large dressing room at the back of the salon.

A shudder rippled through her. *Please don't let it be the Hanover gown.* She visualized rips. She visualized a string of beading cascading to the floor. She visualized Cara's mother realizing that the number on the price tag was a 7 and not a 1 and quickly swiped the credit card.

Drawing a deep breath, she returned to the fitting room where she'd left Cara, her mother, her sister, her grand-mother, assorted bridesmaids and the videographer Mrs. Brantley had hired to record a video scrapbook. Cara's mother held the camera as she, Cara and the videographer stared at a tiny screen.

In the background, Beth heard the ebb and flow of a vacuum cleaner.

"Do you hear that?" Mrs. Brantley shouted as whoever was running the vacuum cleaner in the tux shop next door banged it against the shared wall during each pass over the floor.

Oh, yes indeed, Beth heard that. William. She was going to strangle him. She'd told him that the Brantleys had insisted on an after-hours appointment so the salon would be empty and nothing would interfere with the recording.

He knew, he *knew* that sound carried between the two back dressing rooms of their shops. She'd considered putting sound-proof padding in, or something, but that would mean a disruption in business and, well, she didn't want to admit it, but she liked to eavesdrop on an occasional male conversation in the tux shop's dressing room. She'd been known to pick up a few tips on what styles men found attractive. Once or twice…okay, maybe more, she'd steered a bride away from a certain style based on a snippet of overheard conversation.

William listened, too. Every so often, hadn't he given her a heads-up if a bride had a concern about a dress?

Beth waved everyone outside the dressing room and into the main area of the salon where three carpeted pedestals were positioned in front of a bank of mirrors. Before following them, she pounded once on the dressing-room wall with her fist. The vacuum whined to a stop. "I'll talk to you later," she said in the empty room.

The group had gathered by the sofas and cushy club chairs available for waiting fathers or others who shouldn't be privy to the sight of the bride struggling into complex underwear.

"Listen!" Mrs. Brantley ordered dramatically.

The videographer held out the camera and Beth dutifully gave her attention to the tiny screen. Sure enough, she heard the vacuum cleaner start up on the recording. "I do hear a slight hum."

"*Slight* hum?" Mrs. Brantley was in full meltdown mode. After years in the business, Beth was extremely familiar with the signs. "That 'slight' hum has ruined the video scrapbook. The chapter on selecting the bride's dress is second only to the wedding itself. The look of awe and joy on her face when Cara knew she was wearing The Dress brought tears to my eyes. But can we hear what she said? No. No, because of all the noise."

As the bride's mother vented, Beth tried to figure out what to say. It wasn't as though she could dictate to another store's cleaning crew. But she'd tried. Oh, how she'd tried. The truth was that William Seeger, owner of Tuxedo Park Formal Wear next door, was also her business partner.

"The vacuuming has stopped, Mrs. Brantley. Why don't you re-create the special moment now."

"Re-create? *Re-create?* There is no way to re-create the joyful awe—"

"Dear madam, do please sit down." William and his fake British accent had unlocked the front door, made their way through the racks of gowns and were now in the salon.

Fabulous. This was all she needed. *What* are you doing here? she mouthed at him.

"You pounded?" he murmured, then swept past Beth, and zeroed in on Mrs. Brantley.

"I find that life's disappointments are never as dire when one deals with them from a comfortable chair while sipping champagne." William and his British-butler accent led Mrs. Brantley to one of the sofas.

Beth hated when he used that voice. He only did it to annoy her after she'd asked him to class up his act.

She really hated that it seemed to work. Put a man in a tux and add a British accent, and Texas mamas just melted. Go figure. She herself was immune. William irritated her. On purpose. And enjoyed doing it.

Without looking away from Mrs. Brantley, William held out a hand for a glass of champagne, which Beth supplied, and then stepped back and let him do his thing.

Why was it women responded to him? Yes, he looked good in a tux—but what man didn't?

It had fooled her, hadn't it? Regretfully, William lacked any sense of taste, sophistication or elegance himself, which Beth hadn't known before partnering with him because she'd been seduced by a black wool suit with satin lapels and a matching stripe down the side of the trouser legs.

True, they were well-fitted trousers fitted to something worth fitting, but that was beside the point. Or maybe it was the point. Whatever. Even though William was a natural salesman, she should have known better than to go into partnership with a man who'd named his original formal-wear store the Monkey Suit.

They'd both relocated their stores to Rocky Falls from Wanda's World of Weddings for a fresh start—a more elegant, tasteful, sophisticated start. It was why Beth Ann Grakowski now went by Elizabeth Gray and why she asked Bill to go by William. Little touches made such a difference, but William thought she took those things too seriously. Beth thought he didn't take them seriously enough.

"You don't need to hear what she's saying," William assured Mrs. Brantley. "You know your videographer is going to make a collage of clips with music—I've always been partial to 'Thank Heaven for Little Girls' from *Gigi,* myself."

Mrs. Brantley nodded and sipped.

Beth turned away so no one would see her roll her eyes.

"And look—I know what she's saying. 'Oh, Mum. I love it!' And you said, 'My baby. You look so beautiful.'"

"Yes. Yes, I did say that." Mrs. Brantley heaved a great sigh.

Beth stepped forward with the credit card and receipt and offered a pen.

"It's been a long, emotional day for you." William actually patted Mrs. Brantley's hand. Fortunately not the one holding the pen.

Nodding, Cara's mother signed and now it was Beth's turn to sigh in relief. But silently.

They all agreed to come back and order the bridesmaids' dresses another day, and within five minutes, Beth was alone.

Except for William.

Tie loosened, he sprawled on the sofa with a self-satisfied look on his face. It was an appealing face, Beth supposed, although how that substantial nose and those crinkled eyes and the general rumpled effect of the rest of it managed to look attractive, baffled her.

He did not fit her vision of a romantic partner. Frankly, he wasn't fitting her vision of a business partner. She served champagne and he offered his customers beer, thus perfectly illustrating their different outlooks on business and life.

"What are you still doing here?" she asked.

"Rescuin' yer cute li'l butt."

She narrowed her eyes. "You ran the vacuum cleaner on purpose, didn't you?"

"Yes, I did."

"William!"

"Just trying to hurry them along."

"But you jeopardized an important sale!"

"That girl and her mother have been in three times already, and you're exhausted. I could hear it in your voice."

"You were listening?"

"You bet I was." He gave her a stern look. "It's late and you're here all alone."

William had spent his evening in the fitting room that shared a wall with hers to make sure she was safe. If the appointment hadn't dragged on so long, she'd never have known. "You were looking out for me."

A corner of his mouth tilted upward. "I always do."

Now how could she stay angry at him?

William patted the sofa. "Come have a seat, Beth Ann."

"Elizabeth," she corrected automatically. "And I'd better not."

He regarded her a moment before standing. "You'll always be Beth Ann to me."

Thinking he was on his way back to Tuxedo Park, Beth started to enter Cara's dress information into the new handheld computerized ordering units. But William took her by the shoulders and propelled her to the sofa.

"William, I've got work to do," she protested.

"Time for a break." He pushed at her shoulders until she gave in and sat down.

Oh, that felt good.

"Put your feet up."

Beth shook her head as he sat next to her. "It's late."

But when he reached for her feet and propped them on his lap, she surrendered. Weak, that's what she was.

Easing off one of her black pumps, William tsked at the red line where the stiff leather had pressed against her swollen foot. "You should wear more comfortable shoes."

"These look elegant."

"Do you think anyone notices?"

Beth pulled her foot away and sat up. "Yes. Yes, I do. It's all about appearances, William."

He tugged on her other shoe. "You *appear* not to have a life outside this salon."

"Oh, please. So I work hard. You do, too."

"But I also play hard. You don't play at all."

As her shoe hit the floor, Beth realized that she had no idea what William did when he wasn't at Tuxedo Park. If anything, she assumed he used the time to catch up on chores and the minutiae of life like she did. "What do you do?"

"Well, let's see. I belong to a hiking club. I'm also a volunteer guide for Rocky Falls Park."

She'd been expecting him to say he kicked back and took it easy.

"And a couple of years ago, I tried my hand at brewing my own beer. I joined the microbrewers' co-op. Those are the beers I serve next door. The one with the tuxedo on the label is my recipe." He smiled. "I'm kinda proud of that. Lean back."

Stunned, Beth leaned. "Anything else?" There couldn't be anything else, could there?

"I've been known to take off and fish. I also support Prom Pals, the group that provides tuxes to guys who can't afford to rent them." William started massaging her foot. "And I've attended services at all six churches in Rocky Falls."

Beth stared at him. "I had no idea."

"I know." He stared back as he worked on her foot, flexing it to stretch her Achilles' tendon.

"Why didn't you ever mention any of that?"

"You never asked."

"How was I to know? You should have said something!"

He moved to the other foot. "You're only interested in William. That's Bill's life."

"You *are* Bill."

"Exactly. I am not William. He's this starchy formal character you created."

Beth opened and closed her mouth. Clearly, William had issues with their business model. "You want me to call you Bill? Is that it?"

"I want you to *think* of me as Bill."

"I don't understand."

"Then it's time I explained it to you."

"But—"

"Relax," he murmured, and his fingers began to work their magic.

The tension of the day melted beneath his warm hands. He slowly stroked her ankles and calves before gripping her feet and squeezing all the numb places on her toes.

"Ooooh, you give the best foot rubs." Closing her eyes, Beth sighed and went limp—for just a moment—against the sofa. "Mmm." She settled more deeply into the cushions. "That feels soooo gooooood."

He pulled at the end of her hose so her toes could straighten out. "Oh, yes," she breathed. "Ooooooh, yes."

"You make the sexiest little sounds when I rub your feet," he said.

Her eyes shot open. "I don't make sounds!"

"You do."

Did she? "Well…if I do, they aren't sexy."

"Yeah, they are." His eyes met hers.

Funny how his eyes weren't as crinkly as she remembered. She waited for him to grin or say something annoying, but his thumbs kept working the aching ball of her foot, a dangerous glint in his blue gaze.

The movement of his hands became more intimate and more caressing and Beth was aware that this was more than just another foot rub.

William—or rather Bill—had rubbed her feet many times before, but he'd never looked at her the way he was looking at her now, and his touch had never felt the way it felt now. Beth was caught in the intensity of his gaze. As his fingers worked the base of each toe, she felt a warmth spreading through her middle.

Uh-oh.

With one look, Bill had made her aware of him as a man. He wasn't supposed to be a man—he was supposed to be her business partner. It was understood that the man/woman thing wasn't a part of their agreement. At least, that's what Beth understood.

Bill? Maybe not.

His blue eyes had gone molten and heavy lidded with desire. Yes, desire. For her. Without saying a word, he was changing their relationship and she didn't know if she wanted that.

Still he watched her as he massaged her foot and ankle, and moved up her calf, stroking and kneading.

Those hands…the confidence with which he touched her…their strength…the caring…

A tiny sound escaped her. It could possibly be considered a sexy sound, if one wanted to think of it that way. Which she didn't, but judging from Bill's flicker of a smile, he did. He had a nice mouth. Why had she never noticed his mouth before? Why had she never noticed *him* before?

"Come play with me tomorrow." His voice was deep and husky and vaguely erotic.

She couldn't just take off. And even if she could, she wasn't sure it was wise. "I can't. We're booked."

"The weekend. Let's rent a paddleboat and spend some of this nice spring weather on the lake."

"Monica Teague is coming in. I should be here."

"She's not booked for the whole weekend."

"Cara Brantley's bridesmaids can't come in during work hours."

"What about Thursday? Friday? We can have lunch in the park." The man just would not give up.

"The Indian-doctor couple is coming in," she reminded him. "You have an appointment with Dr. Sharma, remember?"

Instead of backing off, Bill leaned forward until he was inches from her face. "Then you pick a time." His eyes blazed.

Beth smothered a totally unexpected flare of attraction. "It's difficult to plan—"

"Pick. A. Time."

No. She was *not* aroused by this new forceful William—Bill. She was *not* that kind of woman. Well, maybe a little bit. Okay, all the signs were there—the heart going *bippity-bip*, the heated cheeks, the urge to close the distance between his mouth and hers—but she absolutely could not let him know. Because— because she wasn't ready.

"If we dress the entire Brantley-Varnell bridal party, it'll be our biggest wedding ever and something to celebrate," she hedged.

"Good." Bill leaned back. "I'll take you to dinner."

"I'll let you know—"

"No, Beth Ann." His smile was an intriguing promise. "I'll let *you* know."

1

UNSTRUNG

"THE NEW SYSTEM SEEMS to be working. So far, no glitches."

Lia Wainright smiled in satisfaction at the comment from her boss, Elizabeth Gray, owner of Elizabeth Gray Bridal Salon. Honest to Pete, she'd been trying to get the woman to go electronic for the past two years.

Elizabeth was all about elegance and class and to her, nothing said class like the thick bridal-white paper she and her staff used to write up orders or "record selections."

Lia got the whole upscale theme. And she agreed that the tone of a bridal salon influenced which designers would allow their gowns to be sold there, but maintaining the appearance of class and sophistication so important to Elizabeth Gray had become problematic. Lia didn't think the payoff was worth it. The thick paper they used for orders took up a surprising amount of file space. The copier didn't like thick paper, either. And all the information had to be duplicated onto an order form because the paper was too thick to make multiple copies.

The extra steps had caused errors more than once. Elizabeth caught most of the mistakes because she knew the design and stock number of every dress she carried. They should be doing so much business that Elizabeth *couldn't* memorize all the numbers.

Elizabeth felt electronics weren't elegant. But then Lia had found these beautifully sleek silver and charcoal-gray electronic-input tablets and carefully and painstakingly introduced them to her boss.

Why did it matter to Lia whether or not Elizabeth Gray Bridal Salon went electronic? Because efficiency meant increased stock turnover, which meant more profit, which meant eventually, Elizabeth Gray would need help. Lia's goal was to provide that help and, ultimately, become a partner.

Elizabeth Gray had the ideal setup here in Rocky Falls, Texas. Lia was that rarest of people—a Rocky Falls native. Her parents owned the Wainright Inn, a local institution that had seen its share of weddings over the years.

Lia liked Rocky Falls, the Hill Country weather, the scenery and the artsy shops catering to weekend tourists. This was where she wanted to live, and she wanted to support herself away from her parents. Working at the Wainright had been great for after school and summers between college, but Lia needed to prove she could develop a business on her own. The salon wasn't hers, but she'd been Elizabeth's first employee, and immediately had seen the potential.

The falls and the carefully lush landscaping of the park surrounding them were an increasingly popular choice for outdoor weddings. Elizabeth had the right idea to have a high-end bridal salon in the area and it was genius to partner with Tuxedo Park, the formal-wear store next door.

But Lia knew they could do better.

"The staff has made the transition to the input tablets without any problems," Lia assured her boss. Input tablets sounded more elegant than remote terminals.

The staff, all but one members of the iPod generation, had been thrilled to abandon the pen and paper. They'd made the transition in a matter of minutes.

"Another week or so and I think we can forgo paper backup," Elizabeth said.

Lia merely nodded. Elizabeth thought they were still using

the pen and paper and then entering the information in their units, but Lia had been printing backups from the computer—not exactly what Elizabeth had in mind.

Elizabeth was being overly cautious. Inefficient. And so help her, a bit of a fuddy-duddy for somebody only in her early thirties.

She needed to loosen up and she needed to loosen up with Bill—William—her partner, the owner of Tuxedo Park. The man had it so bad for her and the toe-curling looks he gave her when he thought no one was watching made Lia bemoan the lack of eligible single men in Rocky Falls.

Where all these brides found all these men to marry was a mystery to Lia. But she wasn't going to settle and she wasn't going to worry about it. She was only twenty-five. She had plenty of time.

"Did you verify that all associates downloaded their information before they left for the day?" Elizabeth asked as she always did.

"Yes," Lia replied, as she always did.

"Did you know we're dressing the entire Brantley wedding?"

Lia had not known. "Even the mothers?" *This* was why she'd pushed for electronic efficiency.

"Even the *grandmothers*." A rare smile of triumph creased Elizabeth's face. "They made their final selections this afternoon. The whole wedding party will be wearing pinks ranging from touches of blush on the bridal gown to deep rose on the grandmothers. The photographs are going to be stunning."

Lia's heart actually started pounding. "That's so great." She was already visualizing advertising. The salon needed more big-ticket weddings like this. And an entire party willing to coordinate was every bridal designer and salon's dream.

"Yes. It is. It really is." Elizabeth exhaled and removed the scarf from around her neck.

All associates wore black suits and Elizabeth, and only Elizabeth, wore a tie or scarf. Lia had rarely seen her neck.

"We will monitor the selections very closely and I'm counting on you to impress upon the manufacturer how important this order is."

She reached for her collar and unbuttoned the top button.

Whoa. And then she unbuttoned the second one, actually revealing a sliver of skin.

She caught Lia staring. "Too much?"

She was serious. The woman was so tightly wound she had doubts about showing two inches of skin.

"For…?"

"William is taking me to dinner to celebrate."

Of course he was. Lia wished she could pour her boss into a sexy little black dress for the poor man.

"We're going to the Wainright Inn—are your folks at home, or is your dad still off on the wine-buying trip?"

"He's just back. Let me call them." Lia whipped out her cell phone. "Soft-shell crab is in season and he found a great wine to go with it."

"Oh, you don't—"

Lia held up her hand. If she couldn't get Elizabeth into the little black dress, then at least she could help William romance Elizabeth this way. "There's a private party tonight, so I want to make sure they keep at least one bottle back for you."

As she spoke to the Wainright sommelier she gestured that Elizabeth should undo one more button.

Elizabeth shook her head. "This isn't a date. William and I will be discussing the vests and cravats he'll have to order for the men. Naturally, we'll want them made of the same fabric."

Poor William.

Poor Elizabeth. Or Beth Ann, as he called her, except Lia knew better than to admit she knew that.

"Wear the lace jacket," Lia surprised herself by saying after she closed her phone.

"I beg your pardon?"

"Wear the lace jacket," Lia repeated. "Think of it as advertising. No one has ordered it because it doesn't look good on the hanger. It's such a great topper for the mothers and grandmothers." Before Elizabeth could object, Lia went to get the sample. The style came in the usual colors, including a black lace over nude, which was what Lia had originally been thinking of.

But that was before she saw the flesh-toned peach over nude.

Holy cow. Her boss's pale skin was an almost exact match. In the warm, carefully muted lighting of the Wainright dining room, Elizabeth wouldn't look as though she wasn't wearing much of anything.

Could Lia convince her to wear it? *Should* she convince her to wear it? In the bright interior light of the salon, it wouldn't look as sexy as at the Wainright. That could be a good thing.

Lia plucked the pale lace jacket from the rack and brought it to her boss. It was a size smaller than the black, but would fit if Elizabeth went without a blouse. "I found a flaw in the black lace, but I love this with your skin tone." Lia briskly removed the hanger and held the jacket out.

When Elizabeth took it and hesitated, Lia added, "Dinner at the Wainright is such a great opportunity to show the jacket. Put it on while I get the right earrings."

In the display case, Lia found the delicate sparkly hanging earrings she had in mind and returned to the dressing area, not sure whether or not she'd pushed her boss too far. But then she thought of William's lustful gaze—William's hot, searing, sizzling, I-know-my-way-around-a-woman's-body gaze… *If a man* ever *looks at me that way, so help me I* will *pay attention,* she vowed.

Elizabeth was tying the ribbon belt on the jacket when Lia returned with the earrings.

Omigod. Lia flipped on more lights before Elizabeth looked up and saw the full effect in the mirror. *I am so ordering that jacket.*

The thing fit her like a second skin and had the perfect V neckline, sexy but not slutty.

Maybe Lia should order it in two colors.

"This is a Clive Hamilton, isn't it?" Elizabeth smoothed the jacket over her hips and checked the rear view.

"Yes. This is the only design of his we carry."

Elizabeth merely nodded before they both heard William at the door.

"Hey, Beth Ann, you ready for a hot time in the old town tonight?"

Elizabeth grimaced and Lia wondered if William fully grasped how much her boss *loathed* it when he said things like that.

"William." Elizabeth closed her eyes.

And because she closed her eyes, she didn't see what Lia saw, which was the stunned expression on William's face when he first caught sight of her.

Lia dimmed the lights and watched his knuckles turn white where he gripped the door handle.

Yeah. She was *definitely* ordering the jacket for herself.

He visibly swallowed. Elizabeth was saying something as she hung up her blouse and suit jacket, gathered her purse and gave Lia totally unnecessary instructions for closing.

As Elizabeth approached him, William's eyes regarded her with possessive intent. Make that possessive, lustful intent.

Maybe not in the old town, but there were going to be hot times tonight.

All kidding aside, Lia *did* want a man to look at her with that same fierce longing—*man* being the operative word. Lia had seen plenty of grooms since she'd begun working here and knew she wanted a mature adult man who understood the give-and-take involved in marriage and was willing to make the commitment.

William was so willing. She sighed a little as he placed his hand in the small of Elizabeth's back and guided her out the front door. Just before the glass closed, he glanced back at Lia and the corner of his mouth lifted.

She gave him a thumbs-up. Not her place, but she didn't care.

2

SMILING TO HERSELF, Lia locked the door and watched until they drove out of sight.

She flipped off the showroom lights and headed to the office, already calculating the cost of the lace jacket once she applied her employee discount.

After inputting the order on her unit, she verified that all the associates had downloaded their orders and then cross-checked with their appointments for the day.

Everything looked just as it should. Lia cleared out the individual ordering units and plugged them in to recharge.

In another hour or so, she'd be able to do a live chat with Zhin, her Chinese counterpart at the manufacturing plant. With the Brantley wedding, she wanted to make certain the entire order was put through together so the dye lots would match.

She went to the kitchen at the back of the salon for a cup of coffee, but changed her mind when she saw the open bottle of champagne.

"We shouldn't serve our clients flat sparkling wine, now, should we?" Lia poured it into her coffee cup and returned to the office to wait until Zhin had arrived at work for the day.

It was funny that Elizabeth insisted on the finest of everything except champagne. Then again, an excellent sparkling wine beat cheap champagne any day. Except, this wasn't exactly an excellent sparkling wine. Either Elizabeth needed to upgrade or Lia shouldn't be drinking champagne out of a coffee cup. Probably both.

Lia idly searched Google for sparkling-wine ratings, and then Asti Spumante and Prosecco, the sweet Italian sparkling wines. Actually, she liked the idea of serving those. It seemed a hipper side of classy. And maybe they should invest in a cappuccino machine. Shopping for bridal and attendant gowns was an exhausting business emotionally and physically. Those beaded dresses could get heavy, and struggling into various girdlelike contraptions to support them gave a girl a workout. Elizabeth didn't provide cookies and tea sandwiches just to be nice, she served them to keep customers from leaving the store and maybe deciding to go elsewhere to shop after having lunch or dinner.

And speaking of…

After a few more sips of champagne, Lia went in search of the shortbread cookies Elizabeth kept on hand.

She heard rustling when she opened the cabinet in the kitchen. Rustling in a place where food was stored was never good. Lia closed the door and kicked it, hoping to scare away whatever she'd heard.

She didn't hear further sounds or find evidence that anything had been raiding the cookies when she looked inside. Okay, then.

Lia grabbed a box of shortbreads shaped like wedding bells and munched as she checked out Clive Hamilton's Web site. Any designer who knew a woman's body the way he did might have other outfits she'd like to order.

Hmm. The cookies were good and her cup was empty and Lia was thirsty. Virtuously, she drank a glass of water before filling her cup with more champagne. Leaning back in her chair, she propped her feet on the desk and the computer in her lap. That's why they called it a laptop, right?

Opening the chat interface, she typed, Zhin, are you there?

Several moments went by. "Late? Ooh, Zhin, you lazy thing. Big night last night?" she murmured aloud.

Elizabeth was impressed with Lia's willingness to work overtime, but the truth was that over the months, she and Zhin had become friends and Lia enjoyed "chatting" with her. Maybe someday they'd even meet.

"Zhiiiiiiin. Where are you?" Lia spoke to herself as she typed. "Big order. Mucho importante. Major buckos. Lots o' pink."

Lia snickered to herself. Zhin prided herself on her English and would incorporate any new word she heard, slang or not. Sometimes those incorporations made Lia laugh until she sobbed and then her typing deteriorated, which tipped Zhin off that she'd been set up. Zhin took her revenge in subtle ways. Like only being available to chat at 2:00 a.m. or something equally hideous.

Hey you, Zhin typed. You're losing your touch.

Nice use of idiom, Lia noted.

So you've got an expensive, big-deal wedding to dress? Zhin typed.

Exactly, Lia typed back. So can we discuss it now and not in six hours? She added a smile emoticon.

Exactly. Gimme the deets. Zhin was getting really good with American English.

Twelve shades of pink from light to dark.

Twelve? They're making a killing.

But Zhin wasn't perfect yet. Lia stared at the screen and then got it. You mean "overkill." Making a killing means making a lot of profit or acquiring much stuff. Didn't it?

You not going to profit?

Yes, but…

Lia stopped typing and reached sideways for her dictionary of slang and idiom. Much better to use a paperback than to get caught looking it up on the Internet. Zhin's computer was networked to hers and once, instead of downloading orders, Zhin had downloaded the slang dictionary Web site Lia had opened. Mucho loss of face for Lia.

Her fingers were pulling the book from the shelf when she heard rustling again. In Texas, rustling like that usually meant giant roaches—enormous flying things that lived in pine trees, unless they found their way inside classy bridal salons.

She thumped the shelf with the book and the noise stopped. But only because it changed to a flap. Flapping sounds were *much* better than rustling sounds, bugwise. Flaps were more likely made by the cleaning crew next door than flying cockroaches.

Her computer chimed the first part of "Shave and a Haircut," signaling that Zhin was logging in to the order section.

Hang on, Lia typed. I want to talk pinks first and verify that the order numbers match the shades we really want before you download the order.

Okeydoke.

These are the twelve pinks. Lia cut and pasted from the order and sent it to Zhin.

Please arrange in order from lightest to darkest, Zhin requested.

In order from light to dark we have Bridal Blush, Blush, Morning Frost—check that one, I think it looks too purply—Ballet Pink, Petal, Petal Blush, Carnation, Shy Rose, Lipstick, Deep Pink, Rose and Vivid Rose. And these are the numbers I have for them. With Zhin, it was best to do words and numbers separately.

Can you get actual fabric samples and eyeball them all together? she asked Zhin when they'd finished verifying numbers and whether or not the shades were still manufactured.

Eyeball=look?

Yes, sorry. This is a serious order. If one of the shades is off, please say so.

BBIAF.

BBIAF? What was that? She chimed Zhin. Nothing. "BBIAF?" she muttered. "BBIAF. What does she think she means?" Lia chimed "Shave and a Haircut" again. And then again. And again. Zhin? Come on. BBIAF? One more chime.

"Be back in a few!" a male voice called, startling Lia into jerking her hands from the laptop.

She hit the edge of the slang dictionary, which smacked into her cup of nearly flat champagne, and ended up knocking both onto her keyboard. As a guitar strummed the "two bits" part of the jingle, the remnants of a moderately priced California sparkling wine fizzed and sizzled over her laptop. No, the wine didn't sizzle—that would be her computer sizzling. In the throes of electronic death, the screen flashed and went dark.

"No!"

"I'm telling you it is. BBIAF is 'be back in a few.'" The voice was male and deep and so loud, it sounded as though he was standing right beside her. He had to be in the fitting room of the tux shop next door.

"I don't care!" she shouted at him.

Turning the keyboard upside down, Lia shook droplets of liquid from it and tried to reestablish the connection with Zhin.

Nothing. The thing was dead. "No. No, no, no, no."

"I'm telling you, it is."

"I'm not talking to you, whoever you are. Go back to cleaning." At this hour, he had to be part of the cleaning crew.

"What happened?"

"You scared me and I knocked my drink all over my keyboard while I was talking with China, thankyouverymuch."

"Bummer."

Bummer? "Oh, it's a lot more than a bummer." Who was she talking to, anyway? She knew the staff next door, but she didn't recognize this voice.

Where was he? Lia stood and walked toward the end dressing room. When she opened the door, she heard soft singing.

I was talkin' to China
And drinkin' a lot.
But I spilled my drink
And then I was not.

"This isn't funny!" She heard rustling. So *that's* what it had been.

"Who the hell are you? *Where* the hell are you?" She was swearing. She never swore. Never. Made it a point not to because Elizabeth fined them for coarse language, as she called it. But sometimes…sometimes it was called for. Like now.

Lia heard strumming.

I was sleepin'
In Tuxedo Park
It's nice and quiet
When it's dark
But then I heard
An angel swear
And I wished
I wasn't here.

Lia inhaled. And exhaled and inhaled again. "You do realize that I'm so angry right now that I am about to punch through this very thin wall and strangle you?"

"I didn't mean to startle you."

"Well, you did!"

"Sorry, darlin'."

In spite of her anger, Lia couldn't help noticing that the rich bass voice vibrated right through the wall and into her middle. Truthfully, slightly south of her middle, but she wasn't going to admit it.

She didn't like big bass voices that sounded like actors picked to play the Almighty in movies and commercial voice-overs.

She didn't like being called *darlin'*.

And she didn't like the way this voice made her strain to hear more and ignore her poor wine-soaked keyboard and—

Zhin. Today's orders!

Lia yelped and scuttled back to the computer. She shook it upside down some more and then tried to reboot.

Nothing.

Okay. No time to panic. She'd just plug into one of the sales associates' units.

Did that work? Of course not. That would have been too easy.

"Oh, come *on!*" She blew on the keyboard and then got one of the portable fans they used when the salon became too warm.

Women experiencing high emotion were hot and she didn't mean sexually. Not to mention most of the mothers were of the hot-flash age. Small fans were in all the dressing rooms. Sometimes more than one.

After turning on the fan, Lia propped the laptop next to it. And stared. And waited. And hoped.

She was going to have to call Zhin. It was far easier for Lia to place an international call than it was for Zhin to get permission to do so. It wasn't easy to actually get Zhin, herself, to the phone, but it was possible. Sometimes. Depending on who answered the phone and how well they spoke English and how well Lia could garble out the Mandarin Chinese phrase Zhin had taught her and she'd written out phonetically.

Yeah, the phrase she'd carefully stored in a flagged file—in her dead laptop.

With a sick feeling, she saw the recharging units the staff had used to record their orders and remembered that she'd erased their contents after she'd downloaded to the laptop propped next to the fan. No backups on fancy, expensive paper. And she'd stopped Zhin from accessing the network because she'd wanted to discuss the pinks first.

"I hate pink," she said savagely.

"What did that poor sweet color ever do to you?" came from the dressing room.

"It's not what it did, it's what *you* did," she shouted. "And stop listening. Don't you have cleaning to do?"

"Nope."

Lia marched over to the back dressing room and spoke next to the wall. "What are you doing in there?"

"Playin' my guitar." He strummed as he spoke.

Lia still didn't recognize his voice. She would have remembered that voice. "Are you part of the cleaning crew?"

"Nope." He plinked out a phrase, repeated it, and then changed a couple of notes.

"Who *are* you? Does anybody know you're there?"

He chuckled. "You do." Strum, strum.

She did not have time for this. "Give me a reason not to call the police."

"You're not a poker player, are you? You should have told me you'd already called the police. Now I know I've got plenty of time to get away or, even worse, come over there and tie you up…empty the till…steal a few wedding gowns… I could get up to all sorts of mischief."

Lia felt no threat from him based on nothing more than his voice and, well, the fact that he'd used the word *mischief*. Not that she'd had any experience with hard-core criminals, but she couldn't imagine them referring to illegal activity as "mischief." "Come on. Who are you?"

"You know Jimmy?"

"Jimmy?"

"He works here. I'm his cousin."

"Oh, you mean James." James was a junior associate at Tuxedo Park.

"Actually, I meant Jimmy. He hasn't been James since he was christened."

Prissy James had a cousin with a voice like his? "That still doesn't tell me what you're doing at Tuxedo Park after hours."

"It's quiet. I can work on my music here without anybody listening. Nobody's bothered me...until tonight."

"*I'm* bothering *you?*" What nerve.

"You're pretty noisy over there."

"I—" She was going to burst a blood vessel. She was. Really. "I *work* here!"

"Which one are you? What do you look like?"

Oh, no. She did not have time to flirt through the dressing-room wall with a deep voice she knew only as "Jimmy's Cousin."

"I look like a desperate assistant manager who just lost the day's orders and is about to be fired."

"Would that be a blond assistant manager?"

Men. "That would not."

"A brunette assistant manager?"

Lia looked at her light brown hair in the mirror. She probably should streak it into something richer, but she didn't want the bother of upkeep. "Probably not." And on that note, she stepped out of the dressing room and into the office. He said something, but she ignored him.

The computer was still dark, but the keyboard had dried. Zhin probably hadn't noticed that they'd lost the connection since she was still gathering fabric samples.

This was the pits. She'd have to call Elizabeth and tell her what happened.

She sighed. Poor William. He had his hopes up, among other things, she'd bet, and he wasn't getting lucky tonight. What a waste of a fabulous lace jacket.

"Helloooooo," a deep voice called.

"Leave me alone," Lia shouted from the desk.

"I'm not gonna do that. You intrigue me."

Lia rolled her eyes and poked at the dead computer.

"Tell me *you're* not intrigued." His voice sounded closer, as though he'd moved to the other side of the dressing room.

"I'm not intrigued."

"If you weren't mad at me would you be intrigued?"

"No."

She heard something brush against the carpet and then, "Golden brown."

3

As the deep voice sounded in the doorway behind her, Lia jumped and banged her funny bone on the edge of the desk.

She rubbed her elbow as he sang, sans guitar, "I dream of Jeannie with the golden-brown hair... Your name wouldn't happen to be Jeannie, would it?"

He grinned down at her, a living, breathing, I'm-oh-so-charming-and-I-know-it country-lite rocker cliché.

One by one, she mentally ticked off the type:

Longish hair carefully cut in a bazillion layers so it would always look just a little shaggy so he wouldn't be accused of trying too hard—check. Bonus check for sun streaks.

Stubble—check.

Devilish half smile—check.

Optional one-sided dimple—check.

A few lines crinkling around his eyes to demonstrate that he'd been around—check.

Long nose and/or prominent nose that had once been broken or had a kink of some sort in it. The importance of an interesting nose on a man should never be underestimated. Perfect noses on men meant bland good looks. The noticeably imperfect nose meant intriguing good looks. Why was this? Lia had no idea, but he had a definite check in the nose department.

Blue eyes—check. Eye color had never mattered to Lia, but blue eyes seemed to always come with this type.

Ability to slouch attractively… She looked at him lounging against the door frame. An A+ slouch. Check.

Button-down shirt with cuffs rolled up—check.

Jeans carefully worn and faded in just the right places—she'd give him a check even though she hadn't seen the rear view because any guy who fit the type this exactly was bound to be wearing a pair that hugged his butt to his best advantage.

Broken-in boots—check.

Voice…here he didn't get a check because the template voice was usually a tenor. When he spoke, this man's surprisingly deep, lush bass pulsed all the way through her like the vibrate setting on a bed in a cheap motel.

Oh, and the attitude. He definitely had the I-can-be-reformed-by-the-right-woman attitude, accompanied by the care-to-try? twist to his mouth. Double and triple check.

As though she was interested in wasting time reforming anyone. He was not her type, except that she hadn't quite found anyone who was her type, and in the meantime parts of her had decided that he would do and were reacting accordingly.

Stupid parts.

"You said you were the assistant manager," he said. "That must make you Lia."

She braced herself against the unwanted vibrations from his voice and said nothing, although she'd never heard her name poured from a man's mouth in quite that way.

"Pretty name for a pretty girl," he offered.

"You can do better than that."

"I can." He smiled his one-dimpled half smile. "But you haven't convinced me to try."

And she wouldn't. She had work to do. She had computers to dry and pinks to order and Chinese phrases to figure out.

And make no mistake, she was aware that she was alone, at night, in the back office of a closed bridal salon with a strange man. Just because she wasn't getting any weird vibes—the ones caused by his voice didn't count—didn't mean all was well. "That's because I want you to leave, Jimmy's Cousin."

"Call me J.C."

For Jimmy's Cousin? Oh, please. "How did you get in here, J.C.?"

Holding up his hand, he dangled a key. Both Tuxedo Park and the bridal salon had the same key, so that explained that. However... "How did you get the key?"

"From Jimmy."

"And does Jimmy know you have his key?"

His smile faded for the first time. Straightening, he said, "Yes." And held her gaze until something in hers told him she believed him.

Nodding to the computer propped next to the fan, he said, "Good luck with that," and left.

Just left. Which was exactly what she wanted him to do.

She turned off the fan in time to hear him lock the front door and thought about checking to see if he'd actually gone out before locking it, but didn't. Instinct told her that she didn't have to worry about him. Instinct wasn't much of a reason, but the way he'd held her gaze and seemed offended when she'd implied that he'd stolen Jimmy's key worked for her.

There was a lot of psychology involved in selling bridal gowns and the most successful sales associates became shrewd judges of character and experts at figuring out subtexts. Lia's instincts had served her well and she had no reason to think they wouldn't this time.

Moments later, she heard J.C. in the Tuxedo Park dressing room. And that was that.

Except that wasn't that. In spite of herself, she strained to hear what he was up to when she should have been concentrating on her computer disaster.

JORDAN CHRISTIAN UNROLLED his sleeping bag on the padded bench in the back fitting room. Going next door to see what Lia looked like had been a bad idea. Bad, bad idea.

Bad, because he liked what he saw. Bad, because she did, too. Bad, because she wasn't going to admit it. Bad, because he was going to make her admit it.

Yeah, he was. Assistant Manager Lia had issued a challenge with her I'm-all-about-my-work attitude and her you-don't-do-it-for-me expression. It had been a long time since Jordan had encountered a challenge he felt like accepting.

And Lia of the red cheeks, the slicked-back ponytail and the buttoned-up shirt all the sales associates wore was one heck of a challenge.

Jordan had used his best stuff on her, too. Little songs—women had fainted over his little songs—the smile, the drawl… none of it'd worked.

'Course, she was mad about frying her computer, but Jordan figured his best stuff wouldn't have worked anyway. Either he was rusty, a very real possibility, or she'd convinced herself that men were a distraction from her career. Maybe both.

He lay back on the sleeping bag and crossed his arms behind his head. When he'd first seen Elizabeth Gray, the owner of the salon, he'd thought she was so tightly wound that when she finally did spring loose, he'd hear the twang wherever he happened to be at the time. As her assistant, Lia was trying to be exactly like her. That was just wrong.

Because he was spending nights here, he'd overheard them talking the past few days, long after the place had closed down and regular folks had gone home to their families. He'd learned that the wedding-dress business was deadly serious, when he figured it would be all smiles and giggles and happiness. That seemed wrong, too.

There had to be a song in there somewhere.

Jordan got his musical inspiration from traveling around the country, working odd jobs and observing people. It kept him grounded and connected to his audience.

He might spend a day or two somewhere, or he might spend

a couple of months, depending on whether he was recognized or not. No timetable, except that he was due back in Nashville next week to start his new CD. If he had a relative to visit, as he did here in Rocky Falls, so much the better. Since he was performing on most holidays, he liked connecting with family when he could.

During his travels, he'd slept in barns, his truck, lots of bed-and-breakfasts, campgrounds and more than a few tacky motels, but he'd never before slept in the dressing room of a store. It was now one of his favorites. He could work on his music without bothering Jimmy in his apartment, and until everybody left, he enjoyed listening to the women talk.

Jordan liked women, but contrary to his ladies'-man image, he avoided the groupies and the singing hopefuls who wanted to latch on to him. That didn't mean he wasn't tempted, but early in his career, he'd learned that one-night stands left him broody and hollow. Women were too often dazzled by Jordan Christian, the singer, and forgot about Jordan Christian, the man.

To be honest, part of Lia's appeal was that she not only didn't recognize him, it wouldn't matter if she did. She wasn't the dazzled type. She also wasn't the type to pull up stakes and follow him back to Nashville thinking he had more time to give to a relationship than he did.

Which made her just about perfect.

Shoot. He wished he had more time here, but he'd have to work with what he had. Music helped him think and he needed to think about what he wanted to do and how he was going to do it. Reaching for his guitar, he propped it on his chest. China. Lia had mentioned China.

Jordan feathered his fingers in a chord and then altered a note that added a vaguely eastern sound. He liked it. As he plinked the strings one at a time, a word faded into his mind. *Butterfly*.

Butterfly
In a cocoon…

They were all about butterflies here. Girls would come, find their dream dress, and for most of them, it would be the most expensive, elaborate and just plain biggest dress they'd ever wear. And afterward, they'd be changed. They'd emerge beautiful, glowing women. Butterflies.

Jordan turned out the light and softly strummed in the dark.

LIA WAS ON HOLD, racking up international long-distance charges. Even worse, she'd stretched the phone base and receiver as far as she could so she could hear J.C.'s voice.

For international calls, she had to use the salon's corded phone, or she would have been sitting in the dressing room instead of standing in the hall outside it.

But she could hear. He was only singing bits and pieces as he worked out his song, but that voice of his just wrapped itself around her and wouldn't let go. She hadn't thought she liked deep voices, but his had grown on her in what? A couple of hours?

And now that she had come to like his voice, she admitted that the rest of him wasn't so bad, either.

Lia groaned. She was not going to get hung up on an itinerant musician. She wasn't. She wasn't going to think about the one-sided dimple or the large hands or the nose or the confidently amused gleam in his eye. She was not going to be attracted to him. Okay, she was going to be attracted to him, but she was going to ride it out, that's what she was going to do.

He sang another phrase, a little louder this time. His voice sounded just like dark syrup and she wanted to lick it up, preferably off him.

She whimpered.

4

LIA WAS ONE determined woman. Jordan had listened to her spend the better part of an hour working her way through a frustrating maze of people to reach her contact, only to discover that her contact had been waiting at the main switchboard ever since she'd discovered they'd lost the computer connection.

He did love a determined woman, especially one who was about to bust with frustration.

Generally, he preferred that a woman was about to bust from another kind of frustration, but until then, he enjoyed hearing Lia talk sweet as anything and then cuss like a cartoon sailor when she was on hold.

He'd never heard someone say "Fudge brownies!" with such savagery before. That was his favorite—fudge brownies. It could make a good song title. Most of her silly curses could. He was keeping a list.

"Lily of the valley!"

A new one. That was a goodie. On his laptop, Jordan switched from his music-notation program to the word-processing file and added "lily of the valley" to such expletives as "dreamsicle" and "shantung." She said "shantung" like two words with the emphasis on the second syllable. If she was really mad, she added "silk" to the phrase, starting quietly and building, "Silk *shan*-TUNG!"

Damn. He was lying here, writing a new song, and falling in serious like with Lia whateverherlastnamewas.

Serious like.

The last time he'd felt the *L* word in any form for a woman, it hadn't gone well. The relationship had degenerated into a tug-of-war over whose career was more important and who was going to have to accommodate whom at any given time. And neither he nor Shanna had been willing to give up what they'd been doing to follow the other one. Shanna had real talent. As did he. So they'd called it quits. Lesson learned.

Lia didn't have a band of her own and concerts booked two years in advance. Lia—

He was getting way ahead of himself. An hour ago, he'd just wanted her to admit she found him attractive. Rattle her cage a little. Now, he wanted more.

Jordan closed his eyes and listened to her speak with pleasantly firm professionalism. He'd bet she was smiling because she'd read that people could hear smiles in your voice. And that would be the only reason she was smiling, because she sure wasn't happy.

He could make her happy. Real happy.

And he'd do it by freeing her inner Lia.

He'd start not at her neck, but by unfastening that straight black skirt at the waist. This woman needed to breathe, breathe deeply and feed her muscles with oxygen. *Then* he'd unbutton a button at her neck—just one—and the buttons at her wrist, because he wanted her to be able to stretch and move.

An image of Lia stretching, catlike, before raising her arms overhead, drifted into his thoughts. He saw her arms slowly rise and her wrists emerge from the long sleeves. The cuffs flapped open. Her fingers flexed. Her wrists rotated. It was like watching a slow-motion video of a growing flower, maturing and opening.

Good Lord Almighty, since when had a woman's wrists turned him on?

In his mind, she lowered her arms and smiled at him. He saw

his own hands touch her shoulders, kneading away kinks and awakening muscles. She exhaled a sigh and tilted her head back. His hand reached forward and unbuttoned another button on her blouse, allowing him to slip his fingers beneath the collar and touch her skin. Warm. Smooth. Soft. As his thumbs massaged the knots beneath her nape, his fingers slipped the bra straps off her shoulders.

Jordan smiled, because in his mind, they were sturdy, utilitarian straps, and then he frowned because they'd left grooves in her shoulders.

Ooooookay. He was fantasizing in *way* too much detail.

He cleared his throat—and his mind—turned the light back on and concentrated on his song.

Which was about her, naturally.

So. He was attracted. He was interested. He was intrigued. And he was most definitely having carnal thoughts.

"Fudge brownies, fudge brownies, *fudge* brownies!"

Jordan chuckled to himself. Definitely carnal thoughts. He leaned his head against the fitting-room wall and listened.

"I know. I know. Yes, I told you not to access the network. It's totally my fault. Zhin! Chill! Your face is fine. And at least we got the pinks. How do they look?"

Silence.

"Yeah, I had doubts about Morning Frost. Go ahead and substitute Morning Blush. I trust you. Well…I'm honored that you're honored."

Silence.

"Really? So they like the idea that much? Wow. I'm… Hey, I've got an idea. Tell them—no, ask them…well, first tell them it would be an honor, and then ask them if they'd pose for a photo we can hang in our salon. We can call them the Chrysanthemum Wedding team."

Jordan could actually hear the Chinese girl chattering through Lia's receiver. Lia must have pulled the phone away from her ear. Jordan couldn't make out what Zhin was saying and wasn't sure whether she was speaking in English or Chinese, but she sure was excited.

Lia was speaking again. "I'm glad they're enthusiastic. I know Ms. Gray will love the idea. Zhin, you've got a good capitalist streak going there.… That was a compliment! I wish I'd thought of that idea myself.… Zhin, stop it. You know, I'll still like you even if we disagree sometimes. Of course I like you! I was just saying that if you ever disagree, don't be afraid to say so."

Silence.

"Actually, I didn't mean right *now*."

Jordan laughed, tried to stop it and ended up with a horrible muffled snort. His ear popped.

"Zhin, I've got to go."

Oops. Lia had heard him.

"I'll let Ms. Gray know what happened and we'll re-create the orders. I'll e-mail you when I'm up and running again."

Should he say something?

He flinched as Lia's voice sounded right next to his ear. "I hope you're enjoying yourself." She walked away.

Moments later, he heard the front of the salon door open and close.

He couldn't help himself. Jordan leaped up and hurried outside to follow her.

He didn't have to run far.

A furious Lia stood outside the shop, cell phone pressed to her ear. "Do you *mind?* This call is going to be bad enough without you listen— Elizabeth? Sorry to bother you." Lia angrily waved him back inside the shop before pressing her finger to her ear.

Jordan shook his head and made a cutting motion over his throat. There was nothing that had happened that couldn't wait until morning. She didn't have to go and spoil William's night out.

He'd seen the way the man had looked at Beth Ann and the expensive suit he'd worn this evening. When a man wore a suit like that on an outing with a woman, he had serious intentions toward that woman. Men noticed the effect. Women noticed the details.

And Jordan noticed the effect details had on women.

"Don't say anything," he mouthed at Lia.

After glaring at him, she turned around.

"THERE'S NOTHING MORE to do tonight."

Lia stared at Elizabeth. The poor woman must be in shock. After Lia had described the disaster, Elizabeth had seemed distracted, remarking that she remembered the orders and proving it by rattling off the brides who'd come in today and their selections and sizes, waving off Lia when she'd scrambled to write them down.

"Do it tomorrow," she'd said. And then, Elizabeth had looked off into space before clearing her throat and announcing that there was nothing more to do. "Just finish up here and go on home." And then she left.

Left. As in left the shop without the orders placed, without the orders even recorded. Left. Left Lia with the drowned computer.

Okay. Okay, think. Calm. Think calming thoughts. But things were already calm. There had been no yelling, although Elizabeth didn't ever yell per se. When she was angry, her words became very distinct and clipped. But Elizabeth had just spoken normally, if somewhat preoccupied.

Lia didn't know what to do. Either her boss was having a breakdown or…

Or nothing. Her boss was having a breakdown. And Lia had let her walk out in that condition.

She ran out the door in time to watch Elizabeth get into her car. Wait a minute. That was William's truck. And William wasn't driving. William wasn't even in the truck. And Holy Merry Mother of Christmas, Elizabeth peeled out of the parking space with an audible screech of the tires.

Lia stared after her as Elizabeth approached a yellow light and gunned the engine, zooming through the intersection.

"Well, now, that looks promising." J.C. stood in the Tuxedo Park entrance. He glanced over at her. "How'd it go?"

"Didn't you hear?"

"Didn't hear much. Couldn't see anything."

She gave him a withering look. "I'm surprised you haven't drilled a peephole."

"Y'all would notice."

Lia turned to go back inside.

"Hey."

She sighed pointedly, but waited.

"You look like the kind of gal who has a tool kit or knows where one is."

She hated being called a "gal." "Yes. Do you need to borrow something?"

"Screwdriver, for starters. I've got an idea. Hang on and I'll be back."

"Oh, joy." But he didn't hear her.

Leaving the door unlocked, Lia returned to the office and began to close up the store. Minutes later, J.C. appeared with a laptop.

"Where did you get that?"

"It's mine. Thought I'd see if I could help you out."

"I appreciate the thought, but all my files are on the hard drive."

JC moved the fan aside and set his laptop next to hers. "Seems like Ms. Gray ought to look into having more than one computer."

"So noted."

J.C. sat in the desk chair—the only chair—and smiled up at her.

What an evil, rotten thing to do. The man had long eyelashes tipped in gold, innocent (ha) blue eyes and an indecent mouth.

"Tools?"

Yeah, he had tools. And knew how to use them. "Um, are you, like, a computer geek?"

"Do I look like a computer geek?"

"Are you trying to?"

"Not very hard."

"Good job."

His dimple appeared. "I know a little bit about computers."

"I'm thinking I should wait for someone who knows a *lot* about computers."

"And I'm thinking you better get me that screwdriver."

"Excuse me?"

"I'm trying to make amends here. You've got a dead computer—what harm can I do?"

Lia knew enough about computers to know that a lot of harm could be done, even on a dead computer. "I'd like to try to recover the data."

"So would I. You gonna get me that screwdriver?"

She got the tool kit.

J.C. unscrewed his laptop and carefully removed the hard drive. "Do not jounce this. Do not sneeze or otherwise breathe heavily in the vicinity. Do not spill your drink on it."

"I'm not an idiot."

"No, but you're excitable."

"Only when there's a reason to get excited."

He gave her a look. "I'll see what I can do."

Lia gave him a look right back. "Please don't."

J.C. began opening up the salon's laptop. "Why? Have you already got somebody giving you reasons to get excited?"

"No, and I'm not looking. Believe me, work is exciting enough."

He shook his head. "It's worse than I thought."

"The computer?" She stared into it over his shoulder, expecting to see a blackened mass of fried computer guts.

J.C. set down the screwdriver. "No, you."

"What are you talking about?"

"'Work is exciting enough'?" He looked pained. "Selling

wedding dresses is so exciting you've sworn off men? Do you not see the irony?"

"I could be seriously disillusioned by the fact that forty percent of those happy brides will end up divorced."

"But you're not."

"No," she admitted.

"So, to be clear, you're really saying you aren't attracted to me."

That was blunt. "Bingo." Technically, it was more accurate to say that she wasn't going to act on her attraction. A transient who fancied himself a singer and was sleeping in a dressing room? Yeah, no.

J.C. grinned. "Fair warning—I'm going to change your mind."

The face...the eyes...the smile...the voice... She was doomed. Doomed. "Don't bother. Really."

"It's no bother. Really."

Ignoring the little quivers his voice caused, Lia waved at the computer. "Will you please finish with whatever you're doing?"

"Yes, ma'am." He lifted her hard drive and set it in his computer.

She saw where he was going. Good idea. Lia hoped it worked. "Have you switched hard drives like that before?"

"Nope."

She couldn't watch. But she did. "How do you know about computers?"

"Since I spend a lot of time on the road, I've had to learn because there isn't time to leave my laptop at a repair place."

"Are you some sort of salesman?" she asked.

He stopped working with the tiny screws as he considered the question. "I suppose I am."

If he had to sleep in dressing rooms, he must not be a very good salesman, she thought.

After J.C. finished installing the hard drive, he said, "Cross your fingers," and booted up his computer.

Lia waited, hardly daring to breathe. And there it was—the

soul and brains of her computer in J.C.'s body. Computer body—case. Whatever.

He gestured to the keyboard and she opened the connection to Zhin.

"Everything is there!" Lia went dizzy with relief. She immediately chimed Zhin and e-mailed her.

Whoo hoo, came right back and an answering chime sounded as Zhin accessed the network and the orders. Lia stared at the icon indicating Zhin was on the network until it sounded a tone and blinked off.

She leaned over the keyboard and typed, Got everything? Yes.

Her knees actually went weak. "It worked. You actually made it work," Lia said to J.C. as she typed her goodbyes to Zhin.

At his silence, she became aware that her breasts were just inches away from his face.

She pretended that she was not aware that her breasts were just inches away from his face and logged off the network.

"Thank you, thank you, *thank* you!" She straightened. "I'm so relieved and so grateful I could just—"

"Kiss me?"

The words hung in the air. "I was going to say burst."

"Let's go with the kiss."

Before Lia could protest, J.C. hooked his arm around her waist and tugged her into his lap, using a neat maneuver with the chair to buckle her knees.

Scooping her hair away from her nape, he cradled her head with one hand and pulled her against him with the other.

And then he kissed her.

5

FOR ALL ITS seeming spontaneity, it was a crafty, well-thought-out move, probably plotted while her breasts dangled in front of his face.

J.C.'s mouth met hers with confident intent, shifted in a series of erotic pulses—she was going to remember that trick—and settled at the perfect angle.

The. Perfect. Angle.

He was in complete control because she certainly wasn't doing anything to help things along. Frankly, this guy needed no help, so she might as well enjoy the trip.

Lia consciously relaxed enough to let him know she wasn't going to lever herself away in outrage, but not enough to signal to him full steam ahead, either. A girl had to have *some* standards, even if they were negotiable standards.

He rewarded her by taking her lower lip in his mouth and sucking gently as he ran his tongue back and forth against it.

Every nerve in her lip woke up. "Hellllllooooo," they purred.

She relaxed a little more, aware that she had slipped backward enough so that instead of being above him as she had been when he'd first kissed her, they were now on a nose-to-nose level.

Her reward, as she expected, was an awakening of her upper lip.

He lifted his mouth from hers and she felt a smidgen of panic that the kiss was over. Panic, because she might just beg for more and that was never good.

"You taste like cookies and wine," he murmured. "Sweet with a little sin mixed in."

Oh, she did like hearing him say that. Her eyes drifted shut as she allowed herself a few sinful thoughts.

Nothing happened for a few beats.

She opened her eyes. "You're thinking of how you can work that into a song, aren't you?"

"Tryin' real hard not to." His eyes crinkled.

"Try harder."

His mouth, his very talented mouth, creased in a slow grin as he settled her more firmly against him. "I think *harder* is the operative word."

Indeed.

Lia sighed.

He parted her newly sensitized lips with a series of open-mouthed kisses that had her melting. Lia was not the melting type. Or so she'd thought. Maybe, just maybe, J.C. was the first man to find her melting point.

She'd never been kissed like this before. Even worse, he made her afraid she'd never be kissed like this again.

As her body continued melting until she resembled a puddle of discarded satin, Lia slid lower in his arms. Sort of, kind of, well, okay, melting against him so she had as much of her body in contact with his as possible. Any woman would. And probably had.

Through slitted eyes, she saw J.C.'s face above hers, his eyes closed, totally in the moment.

Lia always checked out the faces of the boys and men, er, *boy-men* as they kissed her. It was a habit and she wasn't ever sure what she was looking for. Mostly, she saw guys pursuing goals, or actually, one goal. She knew they were thinking to themselves, "Chicks like kissing, so I've got to put up with it now so they'll put out later."

Sometimes, she caught them watching her, gauging whether she was ready for second base. A sure mood killer.

The expression she loathed was the one of painful concentration, as though the guy had memorized some kissing manual and was trying to remember the steps. Swirl clockwise, thrust, parry. Swirl counterclockwise, thrust, parry. Rinse. Repeat. Blech.

But she had never seen the look of a man reveling in the kiss before. J.C. was clearly enjoying himself, but he wasn't lost in the moment, not completely. He wasn't lost because he wanted to remain aware of her feelings, specifically whether she was ready to stop or not.

And she knew this because…?

Because Lia Wainright was finally being kissed by a *man*, just the way she'd wanted to be.

And she liked it. A lot. More than she should, because kissing was about more than technique, even superb technique. She just couldn't remember what else right now.

What would his face look like if he were totally lost in the moment? She'd never know because then she would have other things to think about besides his expression. Except she wouldn't be thinking. She'd be feeling.

And she shouldn't be thinking now. Why couldn't she lose herself in the moment instead of distracting herself by overanalyzing the kiss? Wondering where it was going instead of just enjoying it all on its own?

Abruptly, Lia placed her hands—which she was sorry to note had only been gripping the chair arms—on either side of J.C.'s head and broke their kiss.

His golden-tipped eyelashes swept upward.

Lia Wainright looked this man right in his blue, blue eyes and smiled.

And then she kissed him.

For the next several minutes, Lia Wainright channeled her inner woman. It should have been effortless. It wasn't, which said something about her that she'd examine later. Much later. For now, she quickly returned the awaken-the-lips favor and then went exploring, learning his taste, and what made him hum. *Especially* what made him hum because that's what sent delicious vibrations over her tongue to bump merrily along the way to those parts of her that appreciated vibrations the most.

Lia knew it was time to break the kiss when she became seriously interested in taking her tongue out of the equation and applying his humming *directly* to those parts of her.

Not now. But, for the love of fudge-ripple ice cream, within the near future.

So, trying to hide her reluctance, Lia retrieved her hands from where they'd been wandering along his leanly muscled arms. Slowly, she gentled her kisses, pleased when he responded in kind.

They stared at one another and then Lia said, "J.C., it's time to put your hard drive back into your machine."

THE FOLLOWING MORNING, Lia stepped next door. She didn't even have a face-saving pretext. "James?" She confronted J.C.'s sales-associate cousin. "Or do you prefer Jimmy?"

"Oh." James flushed a deep cherry pink that clashed with the coral shirt, tie and pocket square he wore to prove that men *could* wear pink.

Lia liked James, but James was *not* the man to demonstrate any shade of pink whatsoever. But James and pink weren't the point. His cousin was the point.

James looked ready to bolt.

Lia cut off his escape. "Yes, I have been talking to your cousin. Tell me about him. Hold nothing back."

Panic flashed in James's eyes. "Is he bothering you?"

Define bother, Lia felt like saying. "Not yet."

"Good." James looked visibly relieved. "He's visiting for a few days."

"And?"

"And he'll be gone soon?"

Lia leveled a look at him. "James, is he sleeping in the back dressing room?"

The panic returned and James went into full defense mode. "He wanted to. I told him he shouldn't, but he likes the quiet. He says he can't hear his music when he's around people all the time."

Lia thought of the bits and pieces she'd heard through the wall. "Some music shouldn't be heard."

"You don't like his songs?" James shot her a surprised look. "'Cause women really like his stuff."

Trust me, James, it's not the songs women like. "They have a certain charm. Are there…a lot of women?"

James rolled his eyes toward the ceiling. "Thousands."

"Really."

"Yeah. That's why he takes off and bums around the country all the time. He works odd jobs and writes music."

This was so much worse than Lia suspected. She was attracted to a talentless, mooching bum. Well, not talentless. He sure could kiss.

"Should I tell him he can't stay here anymore?"

And there it was. Her opportunity to send the annoyingly distracting J.C. on his way.

Lia hedged. "Does William know he's living in the fitting rooms?"

"He's not *living,* and it's just the one—"

"James."

James looked across Tuxedo Park to the desk by the entrance where William discreetly oversaw the fittings. It was the same setup as the bridal salon. The desk was empty. As was the bridal salon's. "William is…distracted just now."

Yeah, Lia knew all about that kind of distraction. And speaking of…was that J.C. dressed in a morning coat? With a pink cravat and vest? Helping a client?

At that moment, he threw back his head and laughed, the deep sound rippling across the store and washing up against her. "My man, it is a fact that a woman planning her wedding is a force of nature. Either embrace the elements, or take shelter."

Lia looked at James. James cleared his throat. "He wanted to try working as an associate. He's actually very good."

Yes. Yes, he was. She squinted. "Is he wearing Bridal Blush?"

"I believe so."

While the glory of a pink wedding excited the Brantley women, selling the idea to men already out of their comfort zone with the whole tux-and-morning-suit thing required skill. And perhaps a few beers from Rocky Falls' own microbrewery.

Lia heard a clink. J.C. and the client tapped their beer bottles together and tilted them upward as they drank in long swallows.

It was 9:35 in the morning.

"Beer. It's what's for breakfast," Lia said.

She stared, hoping the sight of J.C. chugging a breakfast beer would lessen his attraction.

It did not.

A couple of beefy guys and the groom's twin emerged from the dressing room and reached for a beer. J.C. waved them off with samples of pink from the salon's order book. He then proceeded to hold up fabric swatches next to their faces as the guys poked fun at themselves and the groom.

"We substituted Morning Blush for Morning Frost," Lia said idly.

"That's what he told me," James replied.

They both watched as J.C. arranged the men, eyeballed the pinks and made assignments. *Then* he gestured to the beers.

Silk shan-*tung,* the man was a natural. Lia drew a shuddering breath she hoped James didn't hear.

He stared at his shoes. "So…?"

"So enjoy your visit with your cousin."

"THAT'S ALL SHE SAID?" Jordan asked Jimmy after he'd had to watch Lia walk out of the tux place while he convinced three former University of Texas football players that they were going to wear pink.

The trick, he'd discovered, was to tell them that the bride was also considering burgundy, which was way too close to maroon, which, with white, was the color of the Texas Aggies, their mortal foe.

After they heard that and drank a couple of brewskis, all was well. Except Jordan didn't drink much and never at this time of day.

He needed a nap.

"She didn't demand that I kick you out."

Jordan smiled. "She didn't, did she? What did you tell her about me?"

"Just that you like to bum around the country and take odd jobs while you write music."

"Jimmy, my man." Jordan laughed, thought about it some more and laughed again. "You didn't tell her who I was, did you?"

"What do you mean? She knows you're my cousin."

"Right." A man could always count on his family to keep his head from swelling too much. Before Jordan could ask anything else, a very young couple timidly approached the empty desk.

"I got this one." Jimmy started toward them and Jordan decided to let it go.

He headed to the office—the place was a mirror image of the bridal salon—and recorded the orders. He didn't mess with the computer system, but wrote the numbers down so Jimmy could enter them later and get the commission. After that, he walked into the same fitting room where he'd been sleeping to clear away bits of paper and pins left by the Brantley-Varnell groomsmen.

Thoughtfully, Jordan stared at the padded bench, the mirror with the raised platform, the hooks in the walls and the tiny round tables with the cup holders where guys could set their beers.

So. Lia hadn't ratted him out.

He was making progress.

6

THE NEW LAPTOP was delivered at lunchtime, not that Lia had eaten lunch. She *had* snacked on cookies, so now she felt sort of sick. But, Dan the man, it had been a crazy day. Lia kicked off her shoes and closed her eyes, too tired to order food.

She hallucinated a hamburger. A lovely, greasy, beefy thing with onions and pickles. Maybe cheese. Maybe not. She inhaled and her stomach growled, prompting a low chuckle.

Her eyes blinked open. "J.C.! Don't sneak up on me like that!"

"Couldn't resist." He set an open bag on the desk and handed her a drink. "I tried to guess if you were a Sprite, Diet Coke or Dr Pepper gal, but nothing seemed to fit. So I got you iced tea."

"You're good." Lia pushed the straw through the lid and took a long swallow. "Unsweetened. Perfect."

"Like you."

She gave him an exaggerated eye roll.

Grinning, he cocked a hip on the edge of the desk and pulled a hamburger out of the bag. "Just practicing."

Any man who knew his way around a woman's lips the way he did got plenty of practice. "Do lines like that actually work?" Lia accepted the hamburger he handed her.

"If not with a gal, then in a song." He reached into the bag, got a hamburger for himself and started unwrapping it.

Lia eyed him. She'd been thinking about him—never a good sign. That had been one heck of a kiss last night, and kisses like that didn't come her way so often that she wanted to throw out the baby with the bathwater, as it were. So he wasn't her ideal match. Maybe he'd be a good reminder of why it was important to stick to one's standards. Or not. "What do you do when you aren't sleeping in dressing rooms and playing around with your guitar?"

Before biting into his hamburger, he said, "I don't always sleep in dressing rooms, but I'm always 'playing around with my guitar.'"

Which told her exactly nothing. "Fine. Be a man of mystery. Don't tell me."

This clearly amused him. "Eat your burger before it gets cold."

She took an embarrassingly huge bite as J.C. said, "If I told you a lot of people actually pay good money to hear me sing my songs, you wouldn't believe me."

Her mouth full of hamburger, Lia shook her head.

"There you go, then." He tilted his head and watched her inhale the hamburger.

She might have felt a flutter or two, except that her stomach was busy with food.

"Thanks." Lia sighed and crumpled up the wrapping to put it in the bag. "Hey! There's a French fry in here!" She ate it. "Evidence that at one time there were more."

J.C. was unrepentant. "I must have missed that one."

Lia laughed as he gathered up the trash and stood.

Was he leaving already? Obviously. But…but he'd *kissed* her. Last night. In this very room.

Lia had been thinking about it all day and now he was here and had fed her and they'd both eaten onions and…he was going to leave without kissing her again?

"I know you're itching to get busy on your new laptop."

Not. At. All.

"Got a favor to ask. A young couple came in today to rent

a suit. He's in the army and is about to deploy and they decided to get married first. They don't have any money. She's just going to wear her church dress and carry flowers."

Lia knew what was coming. "Oh, J.C., I've heard so many hard-luck stories—"

"This is different. They didn't ask. I'm asking. I'm asking you to let her borrow one of the sample dresses. I know you've got some that have been discontinued."

"Which we sell once a year." J.C. had been listening a *lot*.

He gazed at her. "It's an outdoor wedding on Sunday afternoon. Just a simple dress."

Typical man. There was no such thing as a simple wedding dress.

He softened his voice. "Please."

It rumbled against her heartstrings. No fair. One word in that voice and who could deny him anything? Not Lia.

"Okay," she heard herself saying. Lending the samples was against the rules. So against the rules. Something about J.C. made her forget about rules. "And we don't need to bother Elizabeth with this, either."

"Understood. Well, thanks, Lia." His goodbye smile bordered on impersonal. It didn't even have a dimple. How did he do that?

"I'll try to keep the sound down next door." And he left. No kiss. No hug. No see ya later.

And then came the embarrassing realization that he'd left that way on purpose. Last night's kiss hadn't done it for him the way it had for her.

Ouch.

At least he'd let her down easy and very smoothly. She could appreciate that. A clear signal that they were Not Going Down That Road.

Which was what she wanted. Because it was best. Because, tragically, he wasn't the right type for her.

So instead of feeling relieved, why did she want to run after him and fling herself at him?

Come on, Lia. You know getting involved with him would lead to a messy breakup later. Don't put yourself through that. The man had no home, no money and no job. The only talent she'd discovered so far had been his kissing talent. Which was considerable. And he probably had plenty of women who were willing to overlook the no money, no home and no job issues.

Because…because during that kiss, hadn't she?

Lia heard the front door close and J.C. lock it behind him.

That was a close call.

JORDAN COULDN'T QUITE figure out his fascination with Lia until he overheard one of her conversations with Elizabeth the next day. Lia was pulling dresses, as they called it, when Elizabeth asked her why she was showing the less expensive models when the bride's budget was considerably more.

"The mom's body language tells me she can't afford it," Lia answered. "Styles that skip beading around the hem will cut the cost and still give the bride the look she wants."

"Hmm," Elizabeth had said.

"The mom will be thrilled and the bride will still be happy. Positive word of mouth means more brides in the shop," Lia countered. "Besides, it gives me warm fuzzies."

"Well, it's your commission," was Elizabeth's comment.

"Don't worry. I won't spend all my warm fuzzies in one place."

Jordan hoped she'd spend some of them with him. He knew Lia's secret now. Beneath her determined career-girl facade lurked a sentimental woman with a heart like a marshmallow. Right then and there, he'd wanted to go next door and scoop her up in his arms, but she'd just demand that he put her down. Better to stick with his master plan.

Tonight, the plan was to bring her pizza.

As soon as Elizabeth left for the day, Jordan carried a large pepperoni with extra cheese into the salon's office. He also brought his guitar.

Lia was pleased with the pizza, less pleased with the guitar. She eyed it questioningly.

"I've got something to prove. You hurt my pride, woman," he said, but he waited until her mouth was full of pepperoni pizza to say it. That way, she couldn't object when he started to sing.

Pride was a funny thing. Jordan enjoyed not being recognized, but he wanted Lia to like his music and he wanted her to like it without being swayed by his name.

Oh, yeah, and he also wanted her to like *him* without the glitter of fame shining in her eyes. He might be making more progress on that front. Last night, she'd expected him to kiss her, so he hadn't even though he'd wanted to. Really wanted to.

He strummed a chord, sorely tempted to sing one of his best-known songs, "The Angel in My Heart." But that would be cheating, so he sang a phrase of one of his new songs.

"Too many cloudy days…without the sunshine of your gaze…and it's raining in my heart." He slanted a glance at her.

She was staring at her pizza. "Is that one of yours?"

"Yes." He waited.

"It's not terrible."

Just what he wanted to hear. "But it doesn't make you feel like storming the stage and throwing your underwear at me like my thousands of female fans."

Laughing, she shook her head. "It's kind of gloomy."

"I was in Seattle when I wrote it."

"That explains the cloudy days and the heart full of rain. Is the heart full of pain later on?"

"Actually, yes." Irritated, he set the guitar aside and vowed to rewrite the lyrics. He'd been predictable and she'd caught him.

"I'm sorry," Lia said. "I didn't mean to criticize. I admire you for following your dream."

Said very politely. It was a good thing he was already a

success, or he'd give up after encouragement like that. "So, what's your dream?" he asked.

Lia gestured around them. "I want to become part owner or buy Elizabeth out entirely. I was born in Rocky Falls and I've always wanted to stay here."

"You have roots." Jordan had a place in Nashville, but he didn't consider it his home. He didn't really have a home; he had a tour bus.

"I do." Lia brushed her hands over a napkin and crumpled it. "People want to retire here. I'm already here. The town depends on tourists and weekenders, so there are a lot of owner-run businesses and part-time minimum-wage salesclerks. Great for an after-school job, but not for supporting yourself." She looked directly at him. "That's why I'm making the most of this opportunity."

"Fair enough." Jordan smiled, letting his gaze sweep over her and landing on her mouth. He remembered the way her lips had felt on his and the way she'd made a point of kissing *him*. He wanted to make sure it happened again. "Life sometimes offers more than one opportunity at a time."

The slightest of blushes tinged her face. "Sometimes it's difficult to tell the difference between opportunities and distractions."

He raised his eyebrows. "That's what makes it fun." He stood and watched her eyes widen. One step toward her, and her lips parted.

He clenched his fists. Three more steps and he could bend down and kiss her. Or haul her to her feet and kiss her. But not yet. He had to be patient. So he loosened his fingers, took another step and reached for the empty pizza box. "I'll carry this out to the trash with me."

"What?" She blinked. "Oh. Yeah, thanks."

Jordan inhaled and forced himself to pick up his guitar. Patience was killing him.

"J.C.?"

Darned if his heart didn't kick up a notch. "Mmm?"

"Thanks for the pizza."

That wasn't exactly the "kiss me, you fool" he'd hoped for. But he hadn't expected it, either. "You're welcome."

They stared at each other in one of those moments of mutual awareness before Jordan forced himself to walk out the door. Lia might have a marshmallow heart, but he had a marshmallow head.

Keeping to his plan made him irritable and impatient, two qualities that weren't helpful while working as a formal-wear-rental sales associate. Actually, they weren't generally helpful at all, which Jimmy had timidly pointed out to him the next day.

So Jordan had holed up at his cousin's apartment until it was time to bring Chinese food to Lia. Chinese, because he had a little theme going and he was planning to sing her the song inspired by his time in Rocky Falls.

She'd probably hate it.

He knocked on the door of the office. "Hungry?"

Lia's unguarded face lit up when she saw him and a warm rush of desire flooded his senses. J.C.'s hands shook a little with the effort of not touching her.

Yes, he wanted her. But she had to want him, too.

J.C. HAD THE STRANGEST LOOK on his face. Lia couldn't interpret it. "Are you okay?"

He stalked over to the desk and plopped down the bag from Uncle Lee's Chinese Restaurant. "No."

"What's wrong?"

He exhaled. "I was going to sing you the song I wrote while I was here, but I am in no mood for you not to like it."

"Okay."

"So I'm not going to sing it."

She searched for the right thing to say. "But I might like it."

"I'll think about it." He opened the bag. "I got Chinese food because the song has a little Asian flavor to it. After listening to you talk to…"

"Zhin."

"Zhin, it seemed to fit. Anyway, it's called 'Butterfly' because the women come in here and cocoon themselves in white dresses and when they take them off, they're changed. They're starting a new life." While he talked, he set containers on the desktop.

Lia ignored them. "That sounds beautiful. I'd like to hear it." She meant it. J.C. might have actually written a good song.

"Maybe." He handed her a pair of chopsticks. "This wedding-outfit business is more high-pressure than I would ever have believed. I think the dress is so important because it *is* a cocoon. A woman puts it on as one person, and when she emerges, she's somebody's wife. People treat her differently. She'll even have a different name."

Oh, now, that was just great. A sexy man with depth. How was she supposed to resist a sexy man with depth? Not that she'd had to resist anything.

She sighed and ate her dinner. And afterward, they read their fortunes, cleared up the cartons and little unused packets of mustard and soy sauce and J.C. stood to leave.

This time, Lia stood, too.

"Take care." He took several steps before she worked up the nerve to speak.

"Why won't you kiss me good-night?" There. She'd asked.

His back to her, J.C. gripped the doorjamb. "Because I won't want to stop." He glanced back at her. "I like you, Lia. More than I expected."

And he walked through the door.

"I like you, too, J.C.," she said into the empty room. "More than I expected."

LIA DIDN'T RELAX until the next day when she decided that maybe she wouldn't want a good-night kiss to end, either.

As soon as she had the thought, she felt lighter. She could hardly wait for J.C. to arrive with dinner.

Naturally, this would be the night when he didn't bring her dinner.

An hour passed. She couldn't hear him moving around next door.

Had he moved on?

Without saying goodbye?

Quietly, Lia approached the wall in the back dressing room and listened. Silence. She pressed her ear against the mirror. Not even a plink from his guitar.

How...how *dare* he?

Except for the glow of a security light, it was dark inside Tuxedo Park as Lia unlocked the door. So, J.C. had left, but she still wanted to see for herself. Flipping on the reception-area lights, she strode toward the dressing room and immediately noticed that the glow flickered.

Flickered. Security lights didn't flicker. That was fire. J.C. had probably fallen asleep and set something on fire.

Lia ran the rest of the way, grabbing the doorjamb to stop and gape inside.

J.C. reclined on a bank of pillows, a glass of wine in one hand. "Took you long enough. I figured you'd be starving by now."

He'd transformed the men's fitting room into a...blatant scene of seduction.

He'd used yards of tulle to soften the walls, adding pillows wrapped in colorful satins and brocades—vest and cummerbund material, if she wasn't mistaken. The flickering came from bowls of water that held floating candles and gardenias. A bottle of white wine was chilling and a plate of sushi set in ice was on the floor next to him.

J.C. himself wore a tux, unbuttoned shirt and no tie. His feet were bare.

Okay. There was no mistaking this message.

As she stood there gawking, he reached for the bottle and poured her a glass of wine. "You look ready to relax. If you'd like to change, there are some clothes in the fitting room next to this one."

At her raised eyebrows, he added, "Samples."

Lia took the wine and went next door without saying anything. She had no intention of "changing into something more comfortable," as the saying went, but she was curious to see what he'd selected.

After a large swallow of wine, Lia flipped on the light.

Choice number one made her smile—it was a man's tux in her size. Choice number two was a navy satin bridesmaid's gown. Very elegant.

But number three…he couldn't expect her to wear it. The ivory peignoir was from their new trousseau collection. Gorgeous and sheer, it had the whole bed vibe going for it. It was the kind of outfit silver-screen movie divas wore.

Lia sipped her wine. She'd had no intention of changing, but these were yes, no and I-haven't-made-up-my-mind choices. Clever. Much more up-front than she was used to, but it avoided unwanted groping and awkward excuses.

Not that J.C. would grope.

Or that it would be unwanted.

Lia closed her eyes as the frothy peignoir beckoned. A woman knew she was a woman when she wore that. More important, a man knew it, too.

Why shouldn't she just put it on and go enjoy herself tonight? How often did she get an opportunity like this?

Never.

Never had a man gone to this much trouble to get her into bed—or pillowed floor, as the case may be.

Would she get hurt? Not if she expected nothing long-term. Or any term. Not if she looked on this as just a wildly romantic night with a skillful lover.

Lover. Not boyfriend. Not partner. Not even a possible boyfriend. A lover. How incredibly sophisticated that sounded.

She reached for the peignoir, but let her hand fall to her side. No. That wasn't her. And she wasn't going to pretend that it was.

Remaining in her work suit, she started to return to J.C., but stopped. There was a fourth option. A fourth choice. Why not?

Quickly, Lia began to strip.

7

IT HAD BEEN A LONG TIME since Jordan had been uncertain about a woman. Wait a minute. He'd *never* been uncertain about a woman.

He took a long swallow of ice water, determined not to over-indulge with the wine. He wasn't much of a drinker, but he did like a good wine.

He wanted to make love to Lia Wainright, plain—but not so simple. The timing was lousy. He had to move on. He had commitments that wouldn't allow him to stay in Rocky Falls for much longer. It didn't mean he'd never be back, but he wouldn't be back for months.

Lia was smart. Jimmy had told her he traveled, so she'd know what tonight was about—and what it wasn't.

Jordan ate a piece of sushi and rearranged the pieces to cover up the hole. Why was she taking so long in there?

A door opened. "I don't understand why men complain about wearing a tux," he heard. "They're way more comfort-able than what the bride wears."

Lia appeared in the doorway.

He'd hoped for the see-through negligee, but expected the navy gown. The tux was meant as a joke. And a "Man, did you misread the signals" outfit, in case he *had* misread the signals, which he didn't actually believe, but clearly must…have…

Jordan was unexpectedly turned on by the sight of Lia in the tux. She had changed into the pants, shirt and jacket, bare feet.

She'd left open the collar and top buttons with no tie and—he could see—no bra.

Dry mouthed, he watched as she gracefully sank into a cross-legged sitting position, handing him her empty glass as she perused the sushi platter. "Good wine. Is this by chance the new white wine from the Wainright?"

"Yeah."

"You heard me on the phone that night." She glanced up at him.

"Yes." He poured her another glass and allowed his gaze to travel from the top of her head down her tuxedo-clad body to the tips of her toes.

His hand shook as he was seized by a sudden desire to suck her toes. They were painted red. Apparently red toenails were also a previously unknown turn-on for him.

Waiting until his hand was steady, he handed her the wine just as Lia popped a piece of pickled ginger into her mouth.

"I love pickled ginger. Sometimes I wonder if I really like sushi, or just the pickled ginger." She sipped her wine and made a face. "Remind me not to do *that* again. It's not fair to either the wine or the ginger."

Jordan forced himself to smile when all he wanted to do was lean across the platter and kiss her ginger-puckered lips. She was here. Dressed in a tux, but she was here. She'd come to *him*, just the way he'd planned. And now he didn't know exactly how to proceed. That, he had not planned. He watched as she ate another piece of ginger and really wished she'd give him a little direction. He didn't want to be a jerk, but he didn't want to lose out through inaction, either.

As Lia broke apart a pair of chopsticks, she nodded to the guitar on the bench behind him. "Planning to sing me 'Butterfly' tonight?"

"I don't know. Depends on how the evening goes."

"How do you want it to go?"

"Your call." Jordan knew how *he* wanted the evening to go,

but sensed she wasn't totally on board. Disappointment stung him and it was a pretty good sting, too. One that would be sore for a while.

She eyed him as she ate another piece of pickled ginger.

He should have ordered extra.

Wielding chopsticks, he helped himself to a piece of ginger before she ate it all, and then shrugged out of his jacket. If he was simply going to be sharing a meal, he might as well be comfortable, and the candles were making it hot in here.

Too bad they were the only thing.

"My call," Lia mused. She set down her chopsticks and also removed her jacket. "I appreciate that. I do. But here's the funny thing. The take-it-or-leave-it aspect isn't doing it for me. It's kind of—" she waved her hand around "—clinical. And...I suspect that because you move around so much, these take-it-or-leave-it opportunities come your way a lot. True?" Eschewing the chopsticks, she ate a piece of sushi.

"They're nothing but distractions. And I like to stay focused." He leveled a look at her. "I've been focused for a very long time."

"Am I a distraction?"

He knew what she was asking. "You're a connection. A very rare connection."

She studied him and he knew she was trying to figure out whether he was just feeding her a line or being sincere.

Frustration made his throat tight and he popped another button on the shirt.

She did the same, drawing his attention. And that's when he learned something interesting. He learned that tuxedo shirts weren't totally opaque. The cotton-poly blend was a thinner material so the pleating in front wouldn't be bulky. On a man.

Jordan stared at her...pleats. One more button and... And she'd been mirroring him, hadn't she?

Deliberately? Had to be. *Had* to be. Jordan's chest grew tight and he didn't trust himself to speak.

Oh so casually, he removed the cheap plastic cuff links that were supplied with the shirts and rolled up his sleeves. Almost as an afterthought, he unbuttoned another button down his chest. And waited, heart beating like a bass guitar through an amplifier.

Lia began rolling up her own sleeves. Jordan looked away, toying with a smoked-salmon roll and watching her out of the corner of his eye.

She finished rolling up her sleeves and then, as he held his breath, opened a fourth button.

Four buttons open on him looked comfortable. On her it was deadly sexy.

Jordan dropped the chopsticks.

Lia was going for yet another slice of ginger, using her fingers instead of chopsticks, and missed Jordan's intent.

Excellent, he thought. No sharp objects handy.

He pushed aside the sushi platter and plucked the ginger from her fingers.

"Hey!"

He popped it into his mouth and kissed her. Hard.

She tasted hot and spicy and it wasn't just the ginger. However, the ginger had sensitized his lips and tongue and he figured it had done the same to hers.

He softened his mouth and brushed his lips against Lia's. Talk about burning kisses. He licked her lips, wondering whether she would feel the tingling if he licked other places on her body. Imagining her licking *him*.

"Hmm," she murmured into his mouth.

And stole the ginger with her tongue.

The glide of her tongue against his sent him instantly to the limit of his control. It was like driving downhill and finding out he had no brakes.

"Oh, wow," she said. "That was a first."

And Holy Mary Mother of Ginger, it better not be the last. She looked at him and he looked at her because they'd arrived at the moment. In any relationship, there was always the moment, a moment when a couple continued down the road together or took different paths, ate their sushi and said good-night.

The room was totally silent, except for a sizzle as one of the floating candles burned itself out.

This moment was going on too damn long. Jordan's muscles clenched with the effort of holding himself still. Somebody had to take the next step, or make it absolutely clear that she wanted somebody else to take it.

Maybe somebody should indicate that he was more than willing to start things off. Jordan unbuttoned a fifth button, allowing his shirt to gape open.

Lia's attention caught and held.

Jordan wasn't falsely modest. He knew he looked good, but she checked him out so thoroughly, he began to feel objectified. Which, she would be surprised to learn, was not uncommon.

Women saw an image. They rarely saw him. But Lia had never seen the image. What's more, Jordan believed Lia wouldn't ever confuse the two. It made sense—her whole job was all about image.

A half smile quivered as she unbuttoned her fifth button. "I'm not dressed for this," she whispered, releasing the edges of her shirt.

"Oh, yes, you are." Jordan's voice sounded deep even to him.

He reached for her, one hand skimming around her neck to support the back of her head and the other boldly sliding beneath her shirt to cup her breast.

Her eyes widened. "Oh," she breathed faintly.

He held her for a few moments, enjoying the weight of her breast in his hand, giving her a chance to pull away. When she didn't, he traced the inner curve with his thumb, brushing his fingers over her smooth skin. Stroking. Sensitizing.

"Ohh." This time it was a sigh.

Holding his gaze, Lia slid one hand behind his neck and the other beneath his shirt, splaying her fingers over his pecs, copying his position.

Could she feel his heart pound? Surely it was about to jump into her palm.

Then she brushed her thumb back and forth across his nipple.

Jordan smiled. The fingers of his left hand were callused from years of playing the guitar. What they'd lost in sensitivity, women gained in pleasure.

Lia had no idea what she was in for.

Her breathing had quickened in anticipation. He felt her nipple harden in his palm even before he duplicated her actions with his thumb.

Her breath hitched and her fingers spasmed against his chest, her nails digging into his skin.

He wasn't going to mirror *that*.

Instead, he circled and stroked, plucked and tweaked, working magic with his music-roughened fingers.

Lia's hand stilled as her eyes closed and her head fell back. Jordan bent forward and kissed the side of her neck, nuzzling his way across her jaw.

She made a tiny sound and bit her bottom lip.

Jordan started to ease her down onto the pillows.

"Wait." Lia's eyelids drifted open as she drew her other hand to his chest. Smoothing her palms across his skin, tracing his muscles, she whispered, "Nice."

Jordan inhaled when her warm breath tickled across his skin.

Lia stopped and blinked up at him. "I felt your heart beat faster."

"Yeah."

"I did that?"

He nodded.

"Because I'm touching your chest?"

"Because you're you."

AND HE MEANT IT. He had to. A man couldn't deliver a slick line with his heart beating like that, could he?

Lia stared into J.C.'s eyes and saw no guile, no fake anything. She'd never seen fake anything from him.

His hands had dropped away when she'd spoken, and now she noticed he'd clenched them into fists.

He wanted her. A lot.

And she wanted him. A lot.

Moving her hands sideways, she parted the shirt and slid it off his shoulders, down his arms, all the way to those clenched fists.

Shrugging out of the shirt, he reached for her and did the same.

"*Very* nice," he whispered.

"And now *my* heart's pounding." Swallowing, she reached for his hand and placed it near her heart.

"It is pounding."

Truthfully, part of the beating was due to a touch of nerves. "By the way, please feel free to take the lead from here. I...I've read all these power articles on women asking for what they want...but there haven't been any on what to do when they get it."

J.C. gave her a slow smile that sent a whoosh of tingles shooting through her. "They enjoy it."

His voice sent molten warmth after the tingles. She felt as though her blood had turned into fizzy hot chocolate.

And all this was *before* he positioned them amid the silky pillows and took her mouth in a deep kiss.

This kiss was even better than the one before, and she'd thought about that one so much, she'd been afraid she'd exaggerated the memory and nothing would live up to it.

Surrounded by his warmth and scent, she savored the feel of his skin against hers. His hand splayed against her back, holding her close, but not crushing her against him.

And then he hummed softly, the deep sound rippling through her. Her nipples tightened instantly and she rubbed them against his chest as she drew his tongue deeper into her mouth. He stroked a rhythm that had her desperate to get closer.

He shifted and she realized that her fingers were claws on his shoulders, clutching at him so he wouldn't move away. She unclenched them and rubbed at the places where they'd dug into him.

"Sorry," she whispered.

"About what?" he whispered back, and then continued kissing her so she couldn't answer.

When they finally did come up for air, Lia was pretty much incoherent, but not so incoherent that she was unaware of her responsibilities.

"The door," she gasped.

"I locked it while you were changing." He kissed her nose and curled his hand around her breast.

Ooh. "And…and…we need to be responsible…"

He drew back so she could focus on his face. "I have little packets of responsibility hidden in several convenient corners. I hope you weren't talking about any more responsibility than that."

She shook her head. "You know, you can seduce a woman with just your voice. When you speak, I can almost feel the sound touch me," she said dreamily.

He unbuttoned her tux pants. "I'm planning to touch you with more than my voice."

"Yeah. You're going to play me like a violin."

"That would be guitar." J.C. raised his eyes to hers, but didn't stop easing her legs out of her pants and underwear. "I'm going to strum your strings, feather your frets and cross your bridge."

Lia was almost distracted enough by what he was saying to forget that she was now naked on the floor of a men's dressing room.

With a man.

Who was *not* naked. She reached for his waistband, but he moved away.

"Not yet. I want to get the feel of the instrument before I start playing." J.C. ran one hand down the length of her, starting at her shoulder, dipping in at her waist, his gaze following as his hand climbed over her hip and down her flanks until he stopped at her toes.

Lia was struggling to maintain a relaxed pose against the pillows when she was anything but. She wasn't used to such frank appreciation, of being examined as though he'd unwrapped a present and discovered his heart's desire inside.

J.C. touched her foot and she flinched. "Lia, you are strung way too tight."

"I know."

He bent and kissed her lightly on the forehead, her nose, her chin, her throat, the valley between her breasts and her stomach. He hummed against her belly button and she laughed even as she felt the vibrations deep within. "What are you doing?"

"Loosening your strings." J.C. hooked an arm beneath her knees and lifted her legs. Stroking her thighs with one hand, he reached for something with the other.

What? He was going for the responsibility already? Lia propped herself up on her elbows in time to see him holding a piece of ginger. "You're stopping for snacks?"

Smiling devilishly, he brushed the ginger over his lips before eating it and she understood what he had in mind.

No way. Not with the ginger.

J.C. scooted down and parted her knees.

Maybe they should talk about this. Did he know what he was doing?

He did.

At the first touch of his tongue against the juncture of her thighs, she squeaked and immediately clasped her hands over her mouth.

J.C. lifted his head. "You're okay?"

Actually, Lia was a little shocked. "Fine," she managed to say in a high, breathy voice.

"The ginger isn't stinging, is it?"

"I can't even feel…" Lia became aware of a warmth that hadn't been there before. "Oh."

"Is that a good oh or a bad oh?"

A few tingles joined the growing warmth. "Ooooh." Lia sank back onto the pillows. "I knew I liked pickled ginger."

He chuckled and she felt his tongue on her once more, stroking, spreading the tingling warmth.

Lia clutched the pillows as a kaleidoscope of sensations rushed at her. And they were excellent sensations, sensations that she'd never, ever, ever felt before, sensations that set a new bar for sensations.

J.C. not only didn't need a road map, he discovered previously hidden detours. Lia twisted, trying to get closer and farther away at the same time. The warmth exaggerated every stroke of his tongue. It was too much.

But J.C. slid one arm beneath her hips to hold her more firmly against him and the other hand up her abdomen to fondle her breast.

Lia whimpered. *Whimpered.* No man had ever made her whimper before. No man had ever taken her this far, this fast before. She drew a deep breath, trying to slow down. J.C. was the dream lover every woman wanted at least once in her life and Lia wanted her once for as long as possible.

Though she tried to resist, Lia was swept along in a sensual tide. She buried her fingers in his hair and then he hummed, the vibrations detonating a series of erotic explosions within her.

Omigawdomigawdomigawdomigawwwwwwwwwwd… She may have squealed that out loud. She didn't care. J.C. lightly held her as little tremors continued to ripple through her.

Wow. Just…wow.

She lay there panting and limp as J.C. drew himself alongside her and wrapped her in his arms.

"I'm sorry," she managed to say.

"Why?"

"I intended… I wanted it to last longer."

He dropped a kiss on her shoulder. "We're not finished."

"I don't…can't… Once is usually it for me," she admitted regretfully. And it was regretfully. "I mean…I haven't forgotten I owe you, but I'm pretty much done for the evening."

He tilted her chin until she was looking at him. "You are not done. That was just a startergasm."

She laughed unwillingly. "Maybe that's what it was supposed to be, but I'm telling you, it was the big O for me." Mindful of the etiquette here, Lia rolled to her side and unfastened his waistband. "And I'm very grateful."

"Grateful?" J.C. looked insulted. "Woman, you're supposed to be an exhausted, quivering lump of bliss. What is the matter with the men in this part of Texas?" J.C. lifted his hips and helped her slide off his tux pants, leaving him wearing nothing but a pair of boxer shorts printed with guitars, treble clefs and musical notes.

Not what she expected. Lia raised her eyebrows.

J.C. grinned. "I have a collection."

"Your hobby is collecting tacky underwear?"

"People give them to me. It started as a joke and now it's my thing. It brings in big bucks at charity auctions."

"That's…interesting."

"And obviously a mood killer." He whipped the boxers off and tossed them over her head. "Better?"

"So much better."

He was one good-looking man. Which he knew, but wasn't obnoxious about. "Someone should burn all your underwear. In fact, you should never wear clothes. It would be a public service to women everywhere."

"I don't care about women everywhere. I care about you." He gestured. "Do you like the way I look?"

As if he really expected her to deny it. "That's a lotta look."

He gave a crack of laughter and rolled her beneath him. Lia stared up into his blue eyes with the crinkles around them and the passion in them and felt a pang near her heart. She liked him way too much to walk away without getting hurt. So she'd deal with it. Later. Now she'd stay in the moment, especially since the moment involved J.C. saying, "You are beautiful," in his rumbly voice and lowering his mouth to her breast.

As his hands moved over her, Lia was astonished to feel herself respond. She reached for him, but he caught her hand and put it over his shoulder. Her breath was already coming in gasps. He licked and hummed. She groaned and squirmed. And incredibly, she felt her excitement building again.

"J.C.! I—I—" She didn't even know what she wanted to say.

"Let yourself go, Lia," he murmured.

"Not by myself!" She wrapped her legs around his waist.

He stared down at her, his face strained. "It'll be better if you wait—"

"I'm not waiting." Her hand closed around him and he inhaled sharply.

"Lia," he breathed and slid into her just before she climaxed.

His strokes prolonged her pleasure and she was still trembling when he shuddered against her.

"Thank you," she whispered next to his ear.

He raised his head and brushed her hair away from her face. "Don't be so quick to thank me," he said.

"Why not?"

"You're not an exhausted, quivering lump of bliss yet."

She laughed weakly. "How do you know? I'm feeling pretty blissful."

His dimple appeared. "'Cause you're still talking."

And later, after they ate the sushi, and talked, and finished the wine, and Lia was ready to collapse, J.C. played her body in an encore…that left her completely and blissfully unstrung.

8

J.C.'S CELL-PHONE ALARM woke them and it was a good thing he'd set it. They had to clean and vacate the dressing room before William opened the shop.

Lia had a sex hangover. Her first. And the mirrored walls let her know just how bad she looked.

J.C. just looked attractively tousled.

"Stop looking at yourself in the mirror." J.C. dropped his arms around her from behind.

She groaned and covered her face with her hands.

"Now see, you think you look bad. Me, I look at you and feel plenty pleased with myself."

Lia slid her hands down her cheeks. "You're entitled," she mumbled ungraciously.

Without looking at him, she shrugged off his arms and reached for her discarded tux jacket. "I'll get changed and come back and help you clean up."

"Don't worry about it." He watched her. "If you take the dress and nightgown back to the salon, that'll be enough."

Lia nodded, finally meeting his eyes as they stood. "You're leaving soon."

"Tomorrow afternoon." He smiled faintly. "You know that young couple?"

"With the bride in the borrowed sample dress? Oh, yes."

"I'm going to sing for their wedding first. It's at two o'clock in the gazebo at the park. I'd like you to come hear me."

Her eyes widened.

For the first time, she saw a hint of anger in his. "Don't worry. I've sung at my fair share of weddings."

Lia nodded. "I'm sure you'll do fine. I…I think I'd like to say our goodbyes now." Because she was going to be pretty weepy this afternoon.

"Lia, I want to talk to you."

She held up her hand. "Don't waste time telling me what I already know."

"I don't want to leave, but I have to get back to Nashville," he said in the deep voice she'd never forget.

"J.C., please don't say anything." She squeezed her eyes shut. "Just give me a goodbye kiss to remember."

LIA HAD ABSOLUTELY no intention of going to that wedding, but here she was, on the edge of a crowd by the gazebo. She wasn't even going to lie to herself that she was there to keep an eye on the borrowed dress. She wanted to hear J.C. sing. Really sing, not the quiet snatches she'd heard through the dressing-room wall. If she was going to lose him to his dream of making it as a singer, she wanted to know that it was worth the bruises on her heart.

The crowd kept growing and, frankly, some of these people weren't wedding guests. And there was a buzz in the air, a sense of excitement that seemed odd for a simple wedding in the park.

At least the people quieted when the wedding party appeared, but there was an actual ripple of applause when J.C., carrying his guitar, climbed the steps of the gazebo.

The sun gleamed on his blond-streaked hair and flashed as he pulled his guitar into position. And then he began to sing and Lia closed her eyes as the deep voice stirred intimate memories.

He sang "Ave Maria," bringing tears to her eyes. Okay, so she'd underestimated his singing ability. Seriously underestimated it.

When the ceremony ended, he sang "The Angel in My

Heart." Lia recognized the song and it was such a perfect match for his voice, it almost sounded like the recording.

She heard women sighing around her and indulged in a moment of smugness.

The bride and groom refused to leave until J.C. sang another song.

That's when he sang "Butterfly." It was all about life changes and wedding-dress cocoons, just the way he'd said it was. The song was beautiful and she wanted to cry, but not because it was so beautiful. She wanted to cry because she'd tried so hard not to fall for him, but she had anyway. She wanted to cry because they could have had one more night together, but she hadn't answered the phone when he'd called. She'd been afraid that she'd embarrass herself by asking him to stay in Rocky Falls and work at Tuxedo Park.

The crowd was utterly silent as the last chord died away, and then they erupted in applause.

There were calls for J.C. to sing more, but he shook his head, pointed to the white plastic runner and strummed a few bars of the familiar wedding march.

After it was over, Lia bypassed the bride and groom and headed straight for J.C. She had to let him know she'd heard him sing. She had to let him know she understood his dream and that she believed he could make it. And she just had to see him one last time.

She was pushing her way through the babbling crowd when she caught some of the conversations.

"How did she get Jordan Christian to sing for her wedding?"

"I guess she knows him somehow."

"Would it be tacky to ask for his autograph?"

Lia came to a full stop and the crowd eddied around her.

Jordan Christian. *Jordan Christian?* J.C. for Jordan Christian. *Not* for Jimmy's Cousin, even though he was.

Jordan Christian, heartthrob singer with thousands of female fans, which he'd told her, selling out major venues, which he'd told her, traveling, which he'd told her, known for his insistence on traveling around the country working odd jobs while he wrote his music—which he hadn't told her, but his cousin had.

She'd slept with *Jordan Christian*. How could she not have recognized him? How could she have criticized his music? How could she have been such an idiot?

Jordan Christian himself had spotted her and was cutting through the crowd of thousands of female fans—okay, dozens—to get to her.

When he reached her, he took her hand, kissed the back of it, waved to the thousands—dozens—of fans and led her away.

"Keep walking," he murmured. "Don't look back. My truck is the black one right there." He beeped the lock. "When we get close, open the door and hop in. *Don't* stop."

"Uh, I don't think we're being chased by rabid autograph hunters."

"When they start chasing you, it's too late."

They were in J.C.'s truck and away before Lia finished fastening her seat belt.

They didn't drive far—just to the parking lot at the Wainright Inn. J.C. parked in a row of similar vehicles, lowered the windows and turned off the engine. "We can sit here for a while, just to be safe."

"We could actually go inside. This is my parents' place."

He smiled. "I know. I figured if things got messy, you could get help easier."

Lia studied him, trying to match the J.C. she knew with the Jordan Christian she didn't. "Do things often get messy for you?"

"Yes. But I have people who deal with crowds. I don't have my people here."

He had people. "About that… You're Jordan Christian."

He nodded slowly, watching her. "I was never a hundred percent sure whether you knew or not."

"Not."

"Ah."

"You're famous," she pointed out totally unnecessarily.

"Lia, you've never confused the image and the man. Don't start now."

"I didn't *know* the image."

"But you know me. I'm still the same."

Right. "Show me your underwear."

J.C. unfastened his slacks and pulled them aside to reveal white boxers printed with brides and grooms, wedding cakes, doves and hearts.

"Of course." Lia smiled for the first time since she'd realized he was also Jordan Christian.

J.C. hooked and zipped up his pants, stared straight ahead for a moment and then turned to her. "I'm falling in love with you, Lia."

The words she wanted to hear. Too bad he didn't mean them. Even though her heart started thudding hard, she looked away, waving both hands. "Please don't give me the speech. I want the memories of our night together…and maybe the CD of you singing 'Ave Maria,' because you are fantastic, but that's it."

"Lia, I don't have a speech. I'm trying to tell you how I feel and how special you are to me." He lifted his hand, but she jerked her head away.

"Special like the thousands of other women. Yeah, I get it. I know what that night was and you don't have to pretty it up. I'm not going to cling or cry or sell my 'I slept with Jordan Christian' story to the tabloids. You don't have to worry."

Expressionless, he said, "You've got it all figured out."

"Pretty much."

"So…you want that CD autographed?" His voice had turned cold.

She shivered, and not in a good way. "I was going to go buy it myself."

"Hey, it's no trouble." He reached into a box behind him and dug around. "I gave one to the bride and groom and I've got an extra." Pulling out a jewel case, he snagged a Sharpie from the glove compartment and scribbled on the case. Then he tossed it into her lap.

Without touching it, Lia read, "To Leah, You're one in a thousand. Jordan Christian."

It was a calculated insult right down to her misspelled name. "Wow. And all I wanted was the memory."

"That's all most women want. Enjoy."

Lia took in his tight jaw and the way he wouldn't look at her. "Why are you angry? If anyone should be angry, it's—"

"You?" He glared at her. "I tried to talk to you and you shut me off. I called you and you didn't answer. And as soon as I saw you today, I came straight toward you and told you how I felt. You threw it back in my face and asked me for a CD."

He made her sound awful. "You didn't even tell me your real name!"

"I go by J.C. on the road. The Jimmy's Cousin thing was a coincidence."

"I thought—"

"I know what you thought. You've been very clear on the whole one-night-stand issue and how okay you are with it. Well, I'm not okay with it and I never was, which I've been trying to tell you."

Lia felt awful for about two seconds before anger flared. "How can it be anything but a one-night stand? You're leaving!"

"I have to." Jordan took back the hatefully inscribed CD and dropped it into the box. "My concert and recording schedule for the rest of this year and the first quarter of next is pretty much set in stone. I'm scheduled beyond that, but there's some wiggle room." He laced his fingers through hers. "I'm falling in love with you and I want to keep falling in love with you."

Lia was silent as she looked into Jordan Christian's blue,

blue eyes and saw J.C.'s eyes. Hearing the words she wanted to hear and knowing he meant them was just as painful because nothing was going to change. He was still leaving.

"If you feel the same, now would be the time to say so," he prompted.

Lia swallowed and nodded. "But I can't go on the road with you."

"No, you can't. You're rooted to this place and have your own goals. That's part of what makes you Lia, spelled L-I-A."

She smiled briefly. "Then we're not going to have much of a relationship."

"Sure we will, but it'll take work and commitment. I'll come see you when I can and you'll do the same. Gradually, I'll be able to schedule more breaks and shift my home base to Rocky Falls."

Lia began to hope. "You'd do that?"

"Yes," he said simply. "I can't walk away from what I feel. I can't walk away from you."

"I don't want you to. This has been killing me!"

"Ah, come here." He cradled her face between his hands and kissed her.

Lia rested her forehead against his. "You had better be *seriously* committed."

"I am officially off the market."

Lia laughed. "Do you have to send out a press release?"

He groaned. "Trust me, it wouldn't matter. And, Lia, promise you'll ignore the tabloids."

"Why? They'll be talking about Jordan Christian." She smiled into his eyes. "I've fallen for J.C."

1

UNVEILED

"Anji, I can't believe you're doing this."

"Getting married?" Anjali Rawat smoothed her hands down the white wedding dress. It was too plain for her American wedding reception. "This is not the dress."

Jennifer, her roommate all through their medical residency, unfastened the clips holding the dress sample together. "I'm talking about the whole arranged-marriage thing. It's…it's medieval."

Anji laughed. "No one is forcing me to marry Devak Sharma. It is simply the custom in my culture to have our families arrange for us to meet."

"But…you were born in the United States. You're an American." Jenny gestured dramatically to a huge Cinderella-type ball gown hanging in the fitting room. "*This* is your culture!"

"And that is why Devak and I will have a civil ceremony and reception here before we have the religious ceremony in India."

Jenny unzipped the bag protecting the Cinderella gown.

"No," Anji decided even before she took it out of the bag. "It has the drama of what we're looking for, but there must be more beading and ornamentation. Just this side of being overdone. Think over-the-top."

"Anji, as your maid of honor, I'm supposed to keep you from going crazy with the bling."

Anji laughed. "Wait until you see the ceremony in India! Even though this is our American wedding, we must have an important dress or it will be an insult to Devak's family. No bows or flowers or ruffles—it's all about the beading and embroidery and crystals."

"Gotcha." Jenny looked through the wedding dresses the sales associate had selected for Anji to try on. "Here's one." She pulled it off the hanger. "Gosh, it's heavy!"

The door opened and Lia, the black-suited assistant manager, came in. "I'm so sorry I've left you to fend for yourselves. We're really busy today."

"Actually, we prefer it," Anji said. "Right now, we're only selecting the dresses to try on for my family. You'll have plenty to do when they're here this afternoon."

"So how are we doing?" Lia asked.

"Well…these are very lovely dresses—"

"Let me," Jenny interrupted and turned to Lia. "Think sparkle and beads. If you've got some dresses you thought were so ornate no one would ever buy them—bring those. Don't bother with the sheaths and make sure the dress has a train, the longer the better."

"I can do that," Lia said. "Let me take some of these away. Would you try on these gowns—" she pulled a couple aside "—just for the shape?"

Anji nodded.

As soon as Lia had gone, Jenny started in again. "I don't understand. Why get married now at all?"

"It's time. Soon, Devak and I will have both finished our residencies. When our schooling is over, we become householders. It's one's *dharma* to marry, the natural order of life. It's what's right."

"I get that. But can't the natural order go a little slower? A month ago, you didn't even know this guy existed." She helped Anji into the beaded dress.

"The priest studied our natal charts and chose the most auspicious day for marriage. The next one is months away."

"Natal chart…you mean your *horoscope?*"

"No. The natal chart is the alignment of planets and stars at the time of our birth."

"That sure sounds like astrology."

"It's part of our religious calendar. Marriage is difficult enough. There's no sense in picking a bad day for it when you can just as easily pick a good one. And then everyone is pleased."

Jenny was looking at her as though she'd lost her mind. "I just… You're marrying a stranger! Somebody your *parents* picked out." Jenny shuddered. "I've done the parental setup before and who they consider a good prospect and who *I* consider a good prospect…" She shook her head. "Not even close."

Anji smiled. "Devak is not a stranger. My parents have told me all about him. He meets their qualifications and they believe we would be a good match. And trust me, the aunties have put him through a screening process that makes the CIA look like amateurs."

"But what about *him?*" Jenny lowered her voice. "If you're married, you'll have to have sex with him."

Anji laughed. "Well, I hope so!"

"It's sex with a stranger! Okay, I'll admit the whole sex-with-a-stranger thing might appeal to some people, but I've known you a long time and that's just not you."

"We've met and talked and I think we will have a good life together."

Jenny looked at her closely. "Anji, I understand that it's your decision and you wish to honor your family and culture. And you've told me that if you don't like him, that's the end of it. But I remember that day. You were just off a twenty-four-hour shift. You barely had time to change clothes before you went to meet this guy and his family. A few hours later, you came back, told me you were engaged and slept for fourteen hours.

And you haven't seen him since, have you? How do you even know if you like him?"

"We have spoken on the phone and we frequently e-mail and text."

"Did you at least feel…a little zing?"

Anji remembered his kind eyes and the way they'd both laughed when they realized that they were so sleep deprived they were having trouble forming complete sentences. They'd gone into another room in her parents' house where she'd told him what she wanted in a husband and he'd told her what he expected in a wife.

She remembered wishing that there weren't dark circles under her eyes and that she'd had a chance to get her hair trimmed. He'd held her hand when he'd asked if she wanted to make a life with him and she'd felt the strength flowing from it. He'd kissed her on the cheek, lingering a bit, and she'd had an impulse to turn her head and kiss his lips, but she'd stifled it.

That impulse surely counted as a little zing.

And Jenny might make fun of the e-mails and phone calls, but Anji had grown to like Devak more and more.

"Yes." She smiled. "I think we can say there was a zing."

"And I know better than to ask if you two will test that zing before you're married."

"No." Anji shook her head. "There will be no testing."

"That's just so weird. You aren't going to sleep with the man you intend to spend the rest of your life with, but you—" Jenny stopped and walked around to face Anji. "You have never zinged with a man, have you?"

Anji laughed. "You should see your face! I'm no naive girl, Jenny." She laughed again. "I'm a urologist. A man's penis holds no mysteries for me."

"Great. Anji, you've only ever seen diseased penises. What are you going to do when a perfectly healthy penis comes knocking at your—" Jenny gestured. "—'portal of love'?"

"Then I'll open the door!"

Jenny lowered her voice. "Sometimes the door might be locked. Sometimes the door might not be large enough. Sometimes it might be too large. Sometimes you might not like what's on the other side. Wouldn't you rather know that *before* you're married?"

Anji was laughing so hard she could hardly stand. "Don't they teach you correct anatomical terms in sports medicine?"

Jenny stalked around to the back of the dress. "Sex isn't a sport," she grumbled as she used the big clips to adjust the dress. "Ugh. I'm invoking maid-of-honor privilege. No mermaid gown for you, missy!"

Anji agreed. "There's no train, anyway."

"You won't be comfortable showing all that skin in a strapless dress, which cuts out a bunch of styles." Jenny helped Anji out of the mermaid gown. "I like this princess shape with the cap sleeves. Try it."

As Anji stepped into the gown, Jenny remarked, "You do realize you're spending more time picking a dress than you spent picking a husband."

Anji stared at her reflection as Jenny did up the back. What she'd said was true.

She knew everything *about* him.

But she didn't know *him*.

"Hey—no clips needed for this one." Jenny peeked out from behind the dress. "Oh, Anji! What do you think? This is your shape. And talk about a train."

The dress was very flattering and stately. Stately was good. "I like the sleeves for a bit more covered look, you know?"

Jenny nodded.

"And the neckline is open so it will display the jewels I'll receive."

"Aren't you getting a little ahead—"

"I would not expect my parents to allow me to marry without

bridal jewelry or to arrange a match with a family who would not present me with jewels."

Jenny raised her eyebrows. "All righty then. I'm going to find Lia and help her pull dresses now that I know the look you're going for. It's more efficient. And she may need help carrying them."

Anji shut her eyes. She could hear her speech taking on the cadence of her Indian relatives. Jenny was her friend and cared for her. Anji would probably question her, too, if Jenny suddenly announced she was marrying a man she'd just met.

But Jenny didn't spend weeks every summer visiting India. She didn't truly understand the importance of family in Anji's cultural heritage. And Jenny didn't fully appreciate the rigorous screening a boy and girl went through before their families agreed to a match.

This wasn't an impulsive whim. Anji's family had met Devak's and exchanged biodata and family histories. Their star charts were compatible and he was a Hindu and a Brahman, as was she. She'd known all about him before they'd met.

And then when they'd met… Anji remembered again the feeling of strength in his hand and a sense of recognition—kind of a "Yes, here he is, my life mate."

And, of course, there was that little zing.

2

"DEV! HEY, BUDDY!"

"Josh!" Devak Sharma was genuinely happy to see his former soccer teammate. "It's been a long time."

He and Josh had just emerged from fitting rooms at Tuxedo Park and were waiting for the tailor to measure their pants for hemming.

"So, did you become a doctor?" Josh asked. "Man, all you ever did was study."

"Yes. I'm just finishing my residency in orthopedics."

"Just now?" Josh shook his head. "That's a long time."

"I specialized in spinal surgery."

"No way."

Dev laughed. "Yes, way."

"So you mean, like, you cut people open and stuff? You?"

"I couldn't keep setting you up for goals forever. Life is not a soccer game."

"Hey, speak for yourself. I'm a coach at Rocky Falls Middle School."

"Yes." Dev nodded. "I can see you as a coach."

Josh squinted at him. "I'm having a little trouble imagining you as Dr. Sharma. No offense, but I hope I don't ever have to test your skills."

"None taken."

"So what are you doing here? I've gotta rent a monkey suit

for the awards banquet this year. The lady coaches want to spiff it up a little."

"I'm getting married," Dev told him. He'd hardly told anyone because he'd been so busy. And, too, he could barely believe it himself.

"Congratulations, man!" Josh shook Dev's hand and clapped him on the shoulder. "Where did you find some girl you could con into marrying you?"

"My parents arranged it."

"The old parental-setup routine." Josh winced. "I've done a couple of those. I guess in your case it worked. How long have you guys been dating?"

Dev stepped onto one of the carpeted podiums and handed a sheet of paper to the tailor. "We aren't really dating. She's a doctor, too, and we're at different hospitals."

"Well, you must have managed to find time to get together at some point, or you wouldn't be getting married, huh?"

Dev turned as the tailor marked the rest of the hem. "That's right," he said instead of explaining.

Josh would never understand that Dev was relieved and pleased that his parents had found Anjali.

He had tried traditional American dating and he'd had his heart broken. He didn't like dating if the woman wasn't serious about a possible future. It wasn't "fun" for him to invest his time with someone and start to like her if nothing would come of it.

He held out his arms so the tailor could make adjustments in the fit of his white dinner jacket.

When the tailor had finished, Dev said goodbye to Josh, who high-fived him with a "Good luck, man!" and returned to the fitting room where he would change into the white pants he'd wear during the actual ceremony. For the ceremony here in Rocky Falls, he would wear all white, as he would for the ceremony he and Anjali would have in India. Maybe it was not traditional American wedding attire, but to him, it was a mix of Western and Eastern clothing.

Dev sat on the bench that ran the length of the fitting room and took off his shoes. Leaning his head against the wall, he closed his eyes, aware of a feminine babble coming from next door. Lost in his thoughts, he wasn't really listening until, well, until he heard the word *penis*.

That would get a man's attention every time.

"Anji, you've only ever seen diseased penises," he heard.

That had to be Anjali and her friend…Jennifer, was it? There couldn't two Anjis who were urologists. Besides, he knew she was coming here today and he'd thought they might meet for coffee. True, he communicated regularly with Anjali, but they hadn't seen each other since the night of their engagement.

Dev listened, curious to hear his fiancée interact with her friend, thinking he might learn more about the woman with the tired, intelligent eyes with whom he'd agreed to share his life.

Dev turned his head so that his ear pressed against the wall. Jennifer was talking quite a lot, something Anji had said that she did. She was a former cheerleader who'd gone into sports medicine. Briefly, he thought of Josh, but it would be best to leave the matchmaking to their elders.

Sex. They were talking about sex. At least he thought that's what they were talking about. Anji seemed very matter-of-fact about it. Dev didn't know if he liked that or not. He did know that going through a medical residency was a very good form of birth control because residents wanted sleep more than sex.

Still. Did he really want his future wife feeling calm and matter-of-fact about their sex life?

Wouldn't he rather she showed some enthusiasm?

On the other hand, how did he feel about it? Of course he'd considered it. He'd liked her picture, taken at a time when she was clearly more rested than she'd been the night they'd met. She'd told him she was coming off a long shift, as was he.

As for sexual attraction, if he were being brutally honest, he'd been incapable of feeling anything that night. He wasn't much more capable now. And even if raging lust burned through his veins, to quote a priest in his youth, he wouldn't act on it.

Anjali was nice-looking and certainly not repugnant, from what he could remember. Nothing that stood out in a negative way. But he couldn't remember the details he wanted—her hands, for instance. Were her fingers long or short? Was the hair on her arms fine or coarse? Did she have shapely legs? Thick ankles? Narrow waist? And, for sure, her breasts. He didn't have much of an idea of the size of them from the way she was dressed that night. There were more important things to consider in a mate, but there were also less important things.

He hadn't intended to propose that very meeting, but he'd held her hand and felt…and felt that this was the woman to share his life.

After she'd agreed, he'd impulsively kissed her cheek because he'd wanted to breathe in her scent. Dev believed in chemistry. People either had it, or they didn't.

She wore no perfume. He'd smelled the soap from her recent shower and the familiar hospital scents that lingered. But beneath all of that was Anjali, warm with a hint of spice.

The memory stirred him now as her scent had stirred him then. He and Anjali had chemistry, but it wasn't a surprise that she did not know it yet.

What had he just heard her friend say? *You're spending more time picking a dress than you spent picking a husband.*

Wasn't the same true for him?

Compatibility was only one part of a marriage. There was also *kama,* the sexual part and pleasure part. And they'd both been ignoring it.

Dev wasn't going to ignore it anymore.

He heard Jenny leave the fitting room and impulsively knocked on the wall. "Anji?"

After a few moments of silence he heard her voice, much clearer than before.

"Is that you, Dev?"

"Who else?"

"Any number of people. What are you doing?"

Dev started to explain about coming with his parents to meet with her parents, who were all over at the Wainright looking at the space for the reception. But impulsively he said, "I'm knocking at your 'portal of love.'" And then he held his breath for her reaction.

"Oh, no! You heard us!"

"Yes. But I only listened to the interesting parts."

"You should have said something," she scolded, but there was laughter in her voice.

He swallowed against an unexpected emotion. *There was laughter in her voice.* And he was glad. "Are you kidding? I would have missed Jenny's theories of sexual incompatibility."

This time, she laughed out loud. "Jenny is a very good friend."

"Please tell your very good friend that when I come knocking on your 'portal of love' for real, you will gladly fling open the door."

"Devak!"

He grinned. "In fact, you will be desperate to fling open the door."

She squeaked. "Shh! Someone will hear you."

"Then they'll envy you."

"Oh, you're such a great prize, then?"

"Absolutely."

ANJI'S JAW DROPPED. Dev had never spoken to her like this before. She closed her eyes, hearing his voice as he'd said, "Absolutely." Deep. Sure. Utterly confident. And completely unexpected.

Jenny and Lia bustled in. "Anji, you're going to have to

work out if you plan to wear one of these babies," Jenny told her. "They weigh a ton."

Dresses embroidered in gold and silver and heavy with beads and crystals sparkled from within their plastic bags. This was more like it.

"I know you said no strapless," Lia said, "but we can add straps or sleeves or raise the neckline or anything you need." She hung up the dresses she'd brought and surveyed Anji critically. "I want to get you a different foundation garment. You're spilling out of that one," she added as she left the room.

Dev must have heard. Anji blushed a dusky pink.

"Hey, don't be embarrassed. You're got a great rack. Work it, girl." Jenny did a shimmy.

"Jenny!"

"Oh, please." Jenny was unzipping the gowns and checking the length of the trains. "If I had cleavage like yours, I sure wouldn't be covering it up."

"This is my wedding, not a Las Vegas show."

"I know, but what's the harm in making him drool a little?"

"There will be plenty of time for him to drool later. In private."

"Oh, do I wish I could see his face when you let the girls out to play."

"Jenny, hush!" Anji fanned herself with her hands. "You're embarrassing me!" She hoped and prayed that Dev wasn't listening. Surely he had left the fitting room by now.

"Darn it!" Jenny zipped up one of the bags. "I got the wrong size. I was just so excited to find one with an eight-foot train. Be right back."

She passed Lia on the way out.

"Here we go," Lia said briskly, holding up a white lace-paneled contraption. "We're going to try a torsolette instead of the bustier. A torsolette is longer and will cinch your waist and flare over your hips. You'll have such a nice hourglass shape and it will help support a heavier dress." She smiled at Anji. "And this model comes with garters in case you want an extra-sexy look for your wedding night. I'm telling you, men go nuts."

There was a thump that sounded as though someone had dropped a shoe next door. Or fainted. Anji was feeling light-headed herself.

"Let me help you get out of the bustier. There are so many hooks and lacings you'll never manage on your own. You'll have someone helping you dress on your wedding day, won't you?"

"Oh, yes." Dozens of female relatives and soon-to-be relatives. Her mother was going to see her in this thing.

His mother was going to see her in this thing.

"Good. And I know you'll have someone helping you undress that night." Lia efficiently unfastened the bustier with a speed only someone who dealt with complicated bridal foundations every day could achieve.

"Need some help in there, sir?" Anji heard.

"I'm doing great," was the reply. In Dev's voice.

Anji cringed. If he were any kind of gentleman, he'd leave immediately. He had to know she was completely flustered. There were some details a man, even one's future husband, did not need to know.

"You're all flushed," Lia said. "It *is* getting warm in here. Trying on wedding gowns is hard work."

"Yes," Anji agreed.

"I'll turn on the fans while you position the torsolette. Remember to bend over so your boobs will sit properly. We want perky, not droopy."

If Jenny didn't come back and stop her, Anji was going to grab some extra tulle and gag Lia.

Anji was in a full-body flush. A drop of sweat trickled down her spine. "Could I…could I have a glass of ice water?"

"Oh, of course! I apologize for not offering you refreshments sooner. I'll be right back."

She was sweating like a pig. She couldn't try on these gorgeous dresses like this. Stepping directly into the breeze of the fans, Anji hurriedly fanned herself with the torsolette.

"Anji?"

She barely recognized the rough voice. "You heard everything." So much for the mysteries of the bridal toilette.

"Describe the foundation garment she was talking about."

"Oh, Dev—"

"Tell me."

"All right." She used her clinical-doctor voice. "It's a very long strapless bra with boning to cinch me in at the waist and support my breasts. It has places where the dress can hook to it at the waist for added support of the skirt. It's a remarkable piece of engineering."

"But she didn't finish helping you fasten it, did she?"

"Not yet. It's quite warm in here—".

"Drop it."

"What?"

"Drop. It. Drop the bra thing."

"On the floor? Why?"

"I want to think of you standing there half-naked, surrounded by white lacy things as you choose what you'll wear to marry me."

Anji's eyes widened as her pulse increased. This was… He was… She stared at her reflection. Oh, for pity's sake, she looked like a captured maiden about to be ravished.

She'd spent years suppressing her sexual self because she'd chosen to be a chaste bride. Truthfully, these last years of medical residency there hadn't been much to suppress. However, with her wedding approaching, she was going to have to unsuppress. Anjali wasn't naive enough to believe she could just flip a mental switch on her wedding day and be as sexually confident as her friends.

Dev had to realize that, too. He was letting her know that he was thinking of her in a sexual way and she should be thinking of him that way, too.

"Have you dropped it?" he asked.

"No."

"Coward," he accused her softly.

Was she?

Not usually, but this was uncharted territory. A challenge. It wasn't as though he was in the room with her. She was alone. For now. She should get over herself.

"Fine." Anji set the torsolette on the chair, avoiding looking at herself in the mirror. "Now what?"

"Look at yourself in the mirror."

She crossed her arms over her chest and glanced at the mirror.

"They said you were beautiful."

That wasn't exactly how Anji remembered it.

"Are you looking at yourself?"

Why was looking so difficult? "I—"

"Are you?"

Anji swallowed. Any second and either Lia or Jenny or both would walk in. She turned to face the mirror. "Yes."

"What do you see?"

"What do you think I see? I see a half-naked woman, that's what I see."

"A beautiful half-naked woman. Uncross your arms."

How did he know? Anji stared at the wall and the mirrors and studied the ceiling for hidden cameras.

"Did you uncross your arms?"

Why couldn't she do this? She'd been raised to be modest and this was…not modest. But it was a request made by her future husband.

And how did she think she could be naked in front of him if she was too shy to be naked in front of herself? She forced her arms down to her sides. The cooling breeze from the fan tickled her skin.

A woman gazed back at her. A woman who, yes, had a nice rack. She'd never looked at her body in a sexual way before, trying to see it as a man would.

"Did you uncross your arms?"

"Yes."

"Are you looking at yourself in the mirror?" he asked after a pause.

"Yes."

"Slowly slide your hands up your rib cage and cup your breasts," Dev instructed in a low voice.

"I will do no such thing!" Enough. Anji reached for the corset.

"Please." His voice was rough with longing and…arousal?

He was turned on! She, skinny little Anji Rawat with the two thick braids and even thicker glasses, had excited a man with nothing more than words. And without trying. What would happen if she put a little effort into it and played along?

She drew a breath, willing her voice not to quiver. "I'm sliding my palms over my skin." She did so. "It's so soft." No sense in doing this halfway. "And now my hands have reached my breasts and I'm holding them, feeling their weight." Her breath quickened.

"Imagine that your hands are my hands and that I'm standing there behind you, watching your face."

As Dev described the scene, a jolt of desire such as Anji had never experienced shot through her.

Dimly, she was aware of Jenny's voice. With shaking hands, she grabbed the torsolette and sat on the chair, her knees quivery.

"Anji, look what I've got!" Jenny burst into the room and hung up the dress. "They had another version." Quickly unzipping the bag, she gestured grandly. "Ta-da! Check it out—white with an embellished gold lace overlay. There's a gold sash that ties under the bust and trails down the back of the one-hundred-inch cathedral-length train…. Are you okay?"

"I got a little dizzy. Lia is getting some water, but she must have been interrupted."

Lia hurried in while Anji was speaking. "Here you go. I brought you some cookies, too."

Anji gratefully drank the water, but passed on the cookies. It wasn't hunger that had made her dizzy.

As Lia hooked up the torsolette, Jenny asked, "How much sleep did you get last night?"

"You know how it goes. A few hours here and a few hours there."

Jenny pulled the dress from the bag and held out the train. "You know, I'm the Energizer Bunny, but even I need sleep or my patients suffer."

"Yes, doctor."

"Lecture over." Jenny stepped aside. "What do you think?"

The dress gleamed and sparkled in the light. "That's it," Anji whispered.

Lia had finished fastening the torsolette and was being very quiet. Anji caught her reflection in the glass and was surprised to see that she had both hands pressed against her mouth. And were there tears in her eyes?

When she saw Anji and Jenny looking at her, she laughed self-consciously. "I can't believe I still do this." She fanned at her face. "But sometimes, a dress is just so perfect and I have to be careful not to say anything because *I* may think it's perfect, but the bride might not like it." She fanned harder. "Let's get it on you."

It took both Jenny and Lia to help Anji step into the dress and do up the back.

They all stared.

"The short sleeves and the neckline remind me of those tops you wear with your saris," Jenny began tentatively when Anji remained silent.

"*Cholis,*" Anji supplied in a dreamy voice. This was her

dress, a perfect mix of both cultures. The dress she'd wear to marry Devak.

Lia tugged on the shoulders. "We can raise the neckline if you think it's too revealing," she offered.

The tops of her breasts swelled above the bodice. More than a hint, but less than slutty. Anji smiled. "Oh, no. It's perfect just the way it is."

3

DEV HAD TO BUY a navy blue suit to justify staying in the fitting room. It was worth it to have had that intimate interlude with his future wife. And a man could always use a perfectly tailored navy blue suit.

But it wasn't going to be perfectly tailored unless he stopped thinking of Anji half-naked in the fitting room next door long enough so that he could have the pants measured.

He wanted to be able to answer the "Do you dress right or dress left?" question instead of the "Why are you sticking straight out front in the men's fitting room?" question.

He felt more awake and alive than he'd been in months. And his enthusiasm about the wedding had increased exponentially. Before, he'd been happy and satisfied to have found a life mate he'd enjoy getting to know and love. Now, he was surprised and pleased and *really* enthusiastic…until he wondered if she was okay with what had happened. Had she enjoyed it? Or was she disgusted?

Calm down, Dev.

Except he was proud of himself in an entirely adolescent way. It had been too long since he'd thought of a woman to the point that he'd become visibly aroused. *Hey, look at me!* Now, that *would* get him kicked out of the store.

Dev needed to see Anji and talk to her without their families or the chaperone of the day hanging around. Truly, it was ridiculous, since Anji in particular had seen plenty of men's privates. However, it was tradition, and as their schedules so rarely meshed, wasn't worth arguing about.

But Dev wanted time alone with Anji when he could see her face while they spoke. What had been the abstract idea of a wife had become specifically about her. Truthfully, he hadn't thought much about the details of their wedding—weddings. He was involved in his work and showed up when his family told him to.

What did she think about it all? Feelings such as those were not something to discuss in text or e-mail. Their phone conversations usually ended with one or the other of them being paged or yawning with tiredness.

Not much of a courtship.

Just before Dev thought he was going to have to add a pair of gray slacks to his order, he heard the women leave while Anji changed into her own clothes.

He knocked on the wall. "Anji?"

"Dev! I can't believe you're still there."

"I bought a suit so they wouldn't kick me out."

"Ha! Well, I can't stay in this room because it's booked for another bride."

"I wanted to ask if I could see you."

"Are we not having lunch at the Wainright with our families in thirty minutes?"

"I mean alone. To talk. Really talk. To see each other while we speak. Without someone listening and giggling," he grumbled.

"Oh, my, think of the scandal," she said in a singsong voice.

"See me after lunch. Today."

"I can't. All the women are coming back here to choose my gown. And, Dev, don't mention that we've already found it! Jenny and I were just expediting. My mother thinks I was only getting measured so they could have dresses in my size. Not that they do," she added. "They use clips that remind me of the ones used to close bags of potato chips."

"I will want to hear about all of that later." Not a chance. "So you'll show your mother the dress and then we'll meet."

"Oh, no. First, I'll have to try on several dresses that they can reject. Jenny and I have already picked those. After a time, they'll grow bored. *Then,* I come out wearing the dress I like and they'll be so happy and decide that that is the dress I should have. If I come out wearing it first, they won't like it nearly as much."

Women. Dev shook his head. "Then how about after that? We could have dinner together."

"I rode here with Jenny."

"I'll drive you home!"

"All the way back to Temple? That's hours out of your way."

"So what?"

He heard her sigh. "It will be very late and I'll be very tired. It won't be the best time to have an important conversation."

So. She was avoiding him. Not good. He draped the blue suit over his arm. "My grandmother told me a story about a man and a woman who met each other for the first time on their wedding day. They moved into his parents' home and shortly afterward, they were walking to the market together. It was very crowded and they became separated. She couldn't search for him because she couldn't remember exactly how he looked. So she sat on a bench and waited until he found her. It took a very long time because he wasn't sure of her appearance, either." He stood. "I just want to be able to find you if we become separated, Anji."

"We have cell phones, Dev."

She was deliberately missing the point. In frustration, he whipped out his cell phone and punched in her number. He heard a muffled ringing that grew louder as she uncovered her phone and answered it.

"Dev? What are you doing?"

"We need to talk. We are going to talk. If you want to talk in front of our families at lunch, then I am willing to do so.

However, the topics I wish to discuss are not suitable for lunch conversation and you might find it awkward to answer in front of your parents."

"You're blackmailing me!"

"Yes."

"Well, I don't like it."

"Neither do I."

In the silence, he heard Jenny's voice. "Aren't you dressed yet? We're going to be late and your mother will lecture me about my duties again."

"All right, Dev. You win. I'll meet you after we finish selecting my dress." Anji disconnected.

He closed the phone, feeling nothing like a victor.

"YOU ARE GOING to be a most beautiful bride," Anji's mother told her. "Both here and in India. At first, I say to myself, 'Why must there be two ceremonies?' But the legal and the religious—that I understand. The legal work is so very much easier to do in this country."

Anji hugged her mother. "Goodbye, Mom." Her parents were headed home and Anji was going to have dinner with Dev, who would then drive her all the way back to Temple. The idea had not been received well.

She waved to her father in the car. "Tell Dad to drive safely."

"I don't like the two of you going off on your own." Her mother glared at Dev. "My daughter is a good girl." She shook her finger at him. "You will do nothing to dishonor her."

"I will not, Mrs. Rawat." Dev was very deferential. The perfect Indian son-in-law to be.

If her mother only knew, Anji thought darkly. He may have gotten his way this time, but she was going to make it very clear to him that it would not work in the future.

Her mother turned to her. "And you will do nothing to dishonor yourself."

"Yes, Mama."

Her mother looked suspiciously at them, but was apparently reassured.

No kidding. Anji might sound like a shrew before the night was over, but there was no dishonor in standing up for herself. This bossiness was not an attractive side of Dev and she'd decided that this evening was the opportunity to find out if there were any other traits that were deal breakers.

The official wedding invitations had not yet been mailed, so if she needed to back out of this marriage, she could. And would.

That would teach her to make life decisions after a twenty-four-hour shift.

They waved goodbye to Anji's parents.

"You're angry with me," Dev remarked even before her parents were out of sight.

"Ya think?"

"Come with me and I promise to make it all better." He smiled gently.

She was a horrible fiancée. He'd only asked to sit and talk with her and had waited hours for her to finish at the bridal salon. "Sorry," she told him as they got into his car. "I get snappish when I'm tired."

"I'll remember that."

"And I'm certain I'll have occasion to remind you." She leaned her head back. "However, do not think I will be blackmailed every time you want to do something and I don't."

"But it worked so well," he responded dryly.

Anji smiled. She'd made her point. And he'd made his. They would move forward. "Our families are so very happy."

"They each think they've gotten a prize."

"You know what, Dev? They have."

He glanced down at her. She saw affection in his gaze. It wasn't burning passion, but, frankly, she couldn't have handled burning passion right now. Warm fuzzies were just fine.

But when Dev turned into the parking lot of the Wainright Inn, Anji felt disappointed. They'd just had lunch there. Couldn't he have found a different place for their first dinner alone?

She checked her watch. Four-thirty. A bit early for dinner, considering they'd finished lunch only three hours ago. But she *had* expressed concern about a late night when he'd said he wanted to talk.

Fair enough.

Except they walked right past the restaurant to the elevators.

One was standing open. They walked in and Dev punched the button for the third floor, all without saying anything. He only smiled wearily and leaned against the wall of the elevator.

"I didn't know there was a restaurant up here," Anji said.

"There isn't. I booked a private room."

He'd closed his eyes, otherwise Anji might have been nervous. She recognized that look. She didn't need a mirror to know that her face wore the same look.

Exhaustion. Bone-deep, I've-been-running-on-adrenaline-too-long exhaustion.

Neither was at their best. What kind of meaningful exchange could they have?

The elevator opened onto the third and highest floor. There were only four suites on this floor, including the bridal suite, Anji knew. It was where she'd be dressing on her wedding day.

Dev gestured for her to precede him out of the elevator.

He headed to the right, but Anji didn't follow.

Sure enough, he swiped the key card in the bridal-suite lock. He looked back at her. "Come on."

"No." She punched the down button on the elevator.

Dev blinked at her. Then, shaking his head as though to wake up, he ran his fingers through his hair and walked back to her. "Sorry. I should have explained. It was my attempt at a surprise."

"Oh, you don't need to explain. Just because we—" she gestured vaguely "—we had a moment in the dressing rooms doesn't mean that I'm going to hop into bed with you!" She was disappointed in him. Hugely disappointed.

Dev chuckled tiredly. "Oh, now that *is* funny. Let me show you why."

Reluctantly, Anji followed him into the bridal suite. A bottle of red and a bottle of white wine chilled on a table set with a fruit-and-veggie tray with a bowl of hummus. A bread basket sat next to a silver Thermos. "It's tomato soup," Dev said. He ran his fingers through his hair once more and massaged the back of his neck. "I didn't know if you preferred red or white wine, so I asked for a bottle of each."

"It depends on my mood and the weather."

He nodded, but didn't offer her a glass.

"I apologize. I see you were only securing privacy." She sounded so stilted. Too much time with the relatives today.

"That's not all." He took her hand and led her to the bedroom. "I've been thinking about us and how we're always sleep deprived. I wanted to talk with you when we weren't rushing to do something else, or surrounded by people, or ready to drop where we stood. And I wanted to give you a gift." He gestured to the bed. "So, I'm giving you sleep."

"What?"

The bed was already turned down for the evening, the sheets an ivory color that reminded her of the wedding dress. Slowly, she walked forward.

"I splurged on really luxurious sheets and pillows and a blanket for us and had housekeeping make up the bed. The bed itself is a custom-built pillow top that only the suites have."

Did he realize he was waving food in front of a starving woman? Anji drew her hand over the sheets and felt the soft, silky cotton. And so many pillows. She could cocoon herself.

"If we like it, we can order one of the beds for ourselves."

She heard him approach and stand next to her as she stared at the bed. Dev took her hand again. Once more, she felt the strength and confidence she'd felt the night they met. She squeezed back.

"So, Anji, will you sleep with me tonight?"

She started and tried to draw her hand away, but he wouldn't let it go. "And I mean only sleep. Sleep, glorious sleep. Think of it. We both have tomorrow off. We can sleep for hours and hours with no one to wake us up. And then we can talk."

"You did all this for me?"

"Yes. And, I'll admit, for me, too."

She swayed. "But I don't have my things."

His teeth shone whitely against his skin. "You do. Jenny helped me. There's a bag in the bathroom and the hotel supplies robes."

Feeling like a zombie woman, Anji walked into the bathroom and saw the whirlpool bathtub. "Oh."

She was so easy. Seduced by the promise of glorious sleep and a relaxing soak.

Dev picked up a shopping bag and handed it to her. Inside, she saw a toothbrush and toothpaste, along with various toiletries and a new set of her favorite lounging pajamas in a pale blue cotton knit. Jenny's work.

The gray set she had at home was all stretched out and full of little holes and she'd moaned about having to toss them when she married.

There was a note in the bag, written on one of Jenny's prescription pads. "You are so—" underlined three times "—lucky. Take twenty-four hours and call me in the morning. Love, Jenny."

Anji looked up at Dev, who was regarding her with his dark eyes, and felt a rush of affection. "I don't think anyone has ever given me such a thoughtful gift before. Thank you." She exhaled, feeling the tension already leaving her body.

"You'll stay?"

She nodded. "You would have to drag me out."

He smiled and she noticed for the first time that she liked his smiles and that she hadn't seen many of them. "I've already showered, so you can have the bathroom for as long as you like."

Anji looked at the tub. "Dev? Don't wait up."

4
___

HE HADN'T. When Anji emerged from the bathroom after her first bubble bath in more than ten years all limp and relaxed and swathed in her new pajamas and a thick terry-cloth robe, Dev was soundlessly asleep, sprawled on his stomach.

He looked different without his glasses. Much younger. She had a difficult time reconciling this Dev with the man who'd revealed the sensual side of himself earlier.

Yes. About that.

She hadn't forgotten—how could she?

He'd made her aware. Aware of him. Aware of herself. And now she was curious.

She studied Dev as he slept. Or studied what she could see of him. He wore a shirt and she assumed pajama bottoms. Honestly, they could walk around in public dressed this way and people wouldn't give them a second look.

She could see his face by the light of the lamp on her side of the bed. His skin was light, reminding her of tea-stained milk. He had a high forehead, a bold but well-shaped nose and generous lips. Kissable lips.

She'd not taken the time to study the various features of his face this way, just that they worked together well.

He's quite good-looking, at least the left side of his face is.

Did he find her attractive? She'd certainly done nothing to enhance her looks since she'd started her residency. In the mornings, she washed her face with soap, maybe slapping on a little moisturizer, maybe not, and pulled her hair into a messy lump that sat on the back of her neck. She'd given up wearing contact lenses because her eyes protested. Her only makeup was ChapStick, if that counted. On really special occasions she'd attempt to camouflage the ravages of too little sleep by swiping her cheeks with an ancient powder blush she still had. She suspected it didn't help.

And look at him. Men had it easy. All he had to do was shave and if he didn't, some men could still get away with the stubbled look.

She knelt down until their faces were on the same level and tried to imagine waking up with him in the mornings. Going to bed in the evenings. Making love with him.

Anji conjured up her image in the fitting room and the way she'd felt when he'd asked her to imagine his hands on her. Her skin prickled. She felt warmth pool low in her belly and between her legs. Clinically, she knew this was sexual arousal. Physically, she wanted his hands on her right now.

Such a specific desire was new to her, and Anji allowed herself time to experience it. She consciously relaxed her muscles and repeated the image in her thoughts…. Dev's hands sliding up her rib cage and covering her breasts… Her breathing changed, became faster and deeper. She wanted to be touched and she wanted to be touched by Dev.

Impulsively, Anji leaned toward Dev and very gently placed her lips on his. She liked the way he tasted and the way his mouth felt against hers. She felt pleasure and he wasn't even doing anything. She was going to enjoy marriage. She lifted her head. She was going to enjoy Dev.

Taking off the robe, Anji walked around to her side of the bed, turned out the light and climbed in beside him, the bed so large he barely moved.

Her mother would be scandalized, but honestly, this was no

different than sleeping in the physicians' lounge with other residents when she was on call.

Well, maybe a little different.

She'd never wanted to throw off her scrubs and wrap her naked body around one of the other residents the way she wanted to do with Dev right this very minute.

Anji smiled. Her mother was right to be scandalized.

Anji sank into the bed, felt the exquisite sheets caress her cheek and zonked out.

In the dark on the other side of the bed, Dev touched his lips and smiled.

SUNLIGHT GLOWED into the room around the edges of the blackout drapes. It was still very dark in the room, but not pitch-black.

Anji was asleep.

Dev slowly maneuvered onto his side and faced her, careful not to disturb her. He felt drugged by the amount of sleep he'd had. He didn't know what time it was because he hadn't looked at his cell phone and he didn't care.

Although he'd told Anji he'd had the day off, he hadn't— not until he'd called half a dozen colleagues to get his shift covered today. Dev stretched. He'd promised all kinds of trade-offs, so he was in for a rough couple of weeks.

It was worth it.

Last night, Anji had kissed him. He'd barely awakened as she'd pulled away and was sorry he'd missed it. At least he knew it had happened.

She'd kissed *him*. That was a very good sign.

And he wanted to kiss her. Also a good sign, except that he wanted her awake when he did so. He wanted to taste her. He wanted his tongue to dance with hers. He just plain wanted.

He watched her, thinking of lovers who spent hours watching each other sleep.

After about thirty seconds, Dev was bored with watching

Anji sleep. Afraid he'd awaken her if he stayed, he slipped out of the room and closed the door.

Once in the living area, he stretched again and called room service for a pot of tea and the Sunday paper.

After a quick shower and shave in the suite's other bathroom, he opened the sliding doors to the balcony and when room service arrived, had them set up there.

He heard water running when he closed the door behind the bellman.

Anji was awake. Good timing. Thinking to knock on the bathroom door and tell her about the tea, Dev opened the door to the bedroom and stopped when he heard a gasp.

Wrapped in a towel, she stood by the bed, clutching her purse, her hair falling over her shoulders and down her back, nearly to her waist, or where he thought her waist would be. Not very much past that, the towel ended, revealing sturdy thighs and well-shaped legs. Strong and healthy, not skinny and calcium deficient. She probably thought her thighs were too big, but to Dev they were just right. He could prove it to her with statistical ratios, but in his experience, women didn't care about statistical ratios as much as they cared about how they looked in skinny jeans.

She looked the way a woman should. Period.

They were staring at each other. Anji eyed him warily because he probably looked like a lecher.

He should excuse himself and close the door.

Not a chance.

"I was getting the brush out of my purse," she explained.

"Oh."

After several more moments passed when neither of them said anything, Anji set her purse on the bed and pulled the towel more tightly around her, mounding her breasts above the edge.

Dev guessed she didn't know that. He cleared his throat. "I ordered tea. It's on the balcony."

"Thank you. I'll join you in a few minutes."

Leave. Leave now.

He couldn't stop staring at her and hoping she'd let the towel drop and beckon him to join her in the bed. He could almost feel the sheets against his bare skin.

He wanted to see the breasts he'd dreamed about. He wanted to touch them, suckle them, scrape his teeth across them and hear her sounds of passion.

And know that no man had ever caused her to feel that way. So what if it was politically incorrect? The thought of making her feel like a woman for the first time made him feel like a man. He was already as hard as surgical steel. All that was left was to rip off his shirt, beat on his chest and drag her off by her hair.

"Anji…" He took a step toward her.

"No." Her gaze dropped to his surgical steel.

Couldn't she sound regretful?

"You're so beautiful."

"Thank you. It's good that you think so. However, right now, it doesn't matter and it won't sway me." She marched toward him. "I have been saving myself for my husband for a very long time and you are not yet my husband. I have been teased, called names, been the object of bets, told that I am out of touch with society and that coming to my husband untouched doesn't mean anything anymore." She stopped right in front of him, breathing heavily. "But listen to me, Devak Sharma, this is what our religion teaches and I won't forget it just because your penis woke up."

She went into the bathroom and locked the door.

"I didn't ask you to," he called after her.

"You didn't have to," he heard.

"And I wasn't going to!" He stared at the closed door. "But I wouldn't have said no if you had."

ANJI LEANED against the door as her heart rate slowed. Just watching the expressions on Dev's face as he stared at her had aroused her.

It just showed what fourteen straight hours of sleep would do to a person.

She draped the towel on the vanity and regarded her nude body. Closing her eyes, thinking of Dev's face just now, she slid her palms up her rib cage and cupped her breasts.

Her mouth grew dry and she pulled her lower lip into her mouth.

This didn't have to be all or nothing. They could have something.

Anji honestly believed that Dev hadn't intended anything more than sleep and a chance to talk when they were rested. If she'd believed otherwise, she would never have turned off the shower or picked up the towel and wound it around her waist like a sari and left herself bare from the waist up. Nor would she have unlocked the door and opened it a crack and called his name into the darkened room.

"Dev, are you still out there?"

"Yes."

Anji peeked around the door. Dev sat on the bed, his head bowed, hands dangling between his knees.

"We're not going to have sex today."

"I got that. I never intended to frighten you. I'm so sorry. So very sorry."

Laughing softly, she draped her hair so it veiled her breasts, turned off the light and came out of the bathroom. "You didn't frighten me. You excited me," she whispered.

Dev's head snapped up and when he saw her, he shot to his feet.

"I want to know you a little more intimately."

"Tell me exactly what you want, or we'll know each other a lot more intimately."

"Well, first, I want you to take off your shirt."

With breathtaking speed, Dev reached for the hem and pulled the whole thing over his head without unbuttoning it.

He had a broad, lightly muscled chest and trim waist.

Clearly he attempted to keep himself fit, even on a resident's brutal schedule.

He was watching her look at him. She should say something complimentary, but her mood was rapidly cooling. Her initial impulse had carried her as far as it was going to and her natural reserve was returning.

"I'm glad you're not fat," she said.

He grinned as he drew his hands to his waist. The drawstring waist hung loosely on his hips, well below his navel.

"I'm not going to ask you to remove any more clothing," she said quickly.

"That would be best."

His gaze roamed over her, returning so often to her breasts that she consciously had to keep from covering them. Trying to relax, she slowed and deepened her breathing. Her chest rose and fell, sending a lock of hair slithering to one side. Not exactly what she'd planned.

Dev's eyes followed the movement and clung. What did he see? She wouldn't look. She wasn't ashamed, she was shy.

Concentrate on Dev.

Only then did she notice that his hands had dropped to his sides and were clenched into fists. He was breathing as though he'd run all the way up the stairs to their room. His eyes were dark as he raised them to hers. Dark and intense. Focused.

She shivered and more hair fell away. His eyes followed that, too.

She felt the room's air-conditioning on her skin and knew he could see pretty much everything there was to see.

The longer he went without saying anything, the more she wanted to cover herself with her hands.

No. Not her hands—*his* hands. Yes, that was what she really wanted. Except she wasn't sure how to transition from the two of them staring at each other from across the room to kissing and caressing.

He visibly swallowed. "You said the first?" His voice was husky.

"First?"

"You said the *first* thing you wanted me to do was take off my shirt."

She nodded and blurted out, "In the fitting room, you told me to imagine your hands where mine were and the way I felt. I don't want to imagine anymore. I want to know. And I want to know what your lips feel like when you're awake."

Oops.

But Dev didn't seem to notice. He crossed the room to her. "They feel like this." He bent his head and carefully pressed his lips to hers. They were firm, yet soft, yielding without being pillowy or mushy, and he wasn't pressing so hard her mouth went numb, as had unfortunately happened in the distant past. He tilted his head, changing the angle to a better fit. Oh, yes. That was nice. Very nice. He sucked gently. Very, very nice.

Anji wanted more. No other part of them touched. This barely counted as a kiss. It was the chaste kiss between a schoolboy and a schoolgirl.

And then it wasn't.

Dev brushed his lips back and forth, coaxing hers apart. She swayed forward.

Taking her hands, Dev drew them up to his shoulders at the same time he pulled her lower lip between his and sucked gently.

A trembling started deep within Anji's belly and she clutched at his shoulders. Dev spread one hand against her spine and with the other burrowed beneath her hair, pulling it to the back and cupping her head.

He pulled her against his chest, twisting so that her nipples rubbed against his skin.

"Oh!" she said into his mouth.

And he did it again and it was even better.

Dev deepened the kiss. His tongue rimmed the inside of her

lips before sliding into her mouth. She stroked his tongue with hers and rubbed her breasts against his chest again. And again.

He groaned. "You can't keep doing that."

"But I love the way it feels," she protested.

"So do I, which is why you can't keep doing it." He crushed her to him and took her mouth again.

Anji circled her arms around his neck and toyed with the silky strands of his hair.

They kissed for a long time, learning each other's scent and taste until finally Dev touched his forehead to hers and just held her. "They say a couple falls in love about the time their first child is born."

"I think we're ahead of schedule."

"Yes," Dev said. "We are."

He brushed her hair away from her face. With his hands on her shoulders, he urged her to turn around so she could see their reflection in the full-length mirror on the closet door. Her lips were pink and slightly swollen and a flush bloomed across her throat and chest.

Dev's intense gaze made her breasts feel prickly in anticipation of his touch. Or any touch.

Dev brushed her hair aside and kissed the place where her neck and shoulder met. His tongue circled her skin and he nipped it, not strongly enough to hurt, but unexpected enough to make her inhale. "You leave a mark and my mother will see it!"

"Should I leave a mark where your mother won't be looking?"

"I don't want a mark at all!"

"Nothing to remind you of me?"

"As though I would forget you."

"I want you to think of me, Anji. Of us. And when all the wedding preparations become too much and you are ready to scream, think of us like this and know that I am doing the same."

"Dev," she breathed.

Slowly he drew his hands up her rib cage as she clenched her fists at her sides. Her nipples tightened and his lips curved.

"Dev." It was a plea.

When he finally cupped her breasts, she felt a moment of relief before he drew his thumbs across the tips. In the mirror she saw her eyes widen in surprise as desire zinged through her. "More."

He hesitated.

"More!" she demanded.

He kissed the side of her neck.

"More," she pleaded in frustration.

And finally his thumbs moved again.

Anji's breath hitched as feelings she'd only read about took over rational thought. "More," she whispered.

Dev used his fingers to roll and stroke her into mindlessness.

She shifted her weight from side to side as her body swayed on its own.

Her head fell back against his shoulder and she gave herself up to the exquisite sensations, moving against him.

"Anji…" His breath was ragged.

Dev moved closer to her. Through the towel, Anji felt how hard he was.

She was being selfish, thinking of only her own pleasure without a thought to what it cost him. Drawing a shuddering breath, she placed her hands over his to still his fingers.

Her breath came in great gulps.

So did his.

"Yes, you're right. We must stop now." Dev's voice was low and rough. "But we *will* continue this on our wedding night." He moved his hands, sliding them out from beneath hers and turned her to face him. "I look forward to being your husband, Anjali Rawat."

Anji sighed. "Oh, so do I."

5

Six weeks later...

"Now where were we?"

"Possibly standing a few inches to the left," Anji said to tease her new husband.

"I don't know," he mused from behind her as he gazed at their reflection in the full-length mirror. "Something seems to be missing."

"Perhaps a pair of pajama bottoms and a thick, white, terry-cloth towel?"

"I do believe you're right." Dev's naked thigh pressed against hers.

"That towel made my hips look huge."

"I didn't notice," he said dryly. Splaying his hands over her abdomen, he pressed her against him so she could feel how hard he was.

After a three-day wedding celebration in India, where they were never alone, Dev and Anji had left their parents visiting relatives and had spent the past twenty-four hours flying back to the Wainright Inn where they could at last begin their honeymoon.

It would be only a weekend honeymoon, but they planned to make the most of it.

Anji was already supremely happy. She had only to look at Dev and know what he was thinking. It was very easy, since she'd been thinking the same thing: they wanted to be back in the bridal suite at the Wainright Inn to finish the intimate exploration they'd begun several weeks earlier. And now, at last, they were.

As Dev had on that day weeks ago, he kissed the spot where her neck joined her shoulder and drew his tongue in circles over the skin.

"You're not going to— Ouch! What are you doing?"

"Leaving you a love bite to think of me. When your mother sees it, she will be satisfied that her daughter has made a good marriage, and my mother will be happy she has raised a virile son."

"That is not how virility is proved," Anji said primly.

"I'll get around to the other way momentarily." He sucked on her shoulder.

"Stop that! Where have you gotten these ideas?"

"The *Kama Sutra* is big on biting and marking and scratching with the nails."

"You read the *Kama Sutra?*" She giggled. She couldn't help it. "Dev, you silly man."

He gave her a look that made her reconsider her choice of words. "Our friends have a similar sense of humor. We've received eight copies as gifts."

"Eight?"

"Seven from the doctors I work with, who obviously believe I have spent my entire adult life buried in textbooks, and one from Jenny."

"My Jenny?"

Dev looked irritated. "She was serious, too. Apparently she felt that you had waited such a long time, I had better be fabulous in the sack. She highlighted certain sections for me."

"She did *not.*"

"I was joking about the highlighting, but she did inscribe it with 'Real men read the instruction manual.'"

Anji had to tread very carefully here. "Dev, I'm sure you didn't need to read the *Kama Sutra.*"

"Oh, I don't know. There's an informative section on courtesans."

"Which you will never need. Just remember, you are the man who seduced me with nothing more than words, and enslaved me with only kisses and caresses." Using their reflection as a guide, Anji raised her arm and rested her hand on the back of Dev's neck.

Guiding him down toward her, she turned her head and kissed him.

At the same time, he smoothed his palms over her rib cage and covered her breasts.

Anji reacted immediately with a need so strong she felt it throbbing between her legs. She'd anticipated this moment for weeks and it was as though her desire had never cooled, but had remained banked, always in the background and ready to flare into life.

It had flared, all right. With a groan, she clasped the backs of Dev's thighs and rubbed her bottom against his hard length.

Dev froze.

And…and his hard length became not so hard. Or so long.

Anji had dealt with this problem in her patients, but she suspected Dev was not dealing with a medical issue.

"What's wrong?"

"I don't want to hurt you."

"Then don't." She turned to face him.

"I might not be able to help it since no one—" he smiled faintly "—has gone through your 'portal of love' before."

"Oh, Dev." Smiling, she looped her arms around his neck. "There will be no crying or bloody sheets for you to hang over the balcony to display to the villagers."

He chuckled as she'd meant for him to.

"I'm twenty-nine years old. I've had many physical exams and have worn tampons for years. You don't need to come at me like a battering ram when the door is unlocked." She kissed him and felt him swell against her once more.

"The door may be unlocked, but I'm going to grease the hinges." Dev picked her up and carried her over to the bed. Setting her on it, he captured her wrists and held them above her head. Starting at her forehead, he kissed and nibbled and licked his way down her body.

Anji had been so matter-of-factly confident. She was an idiot. There was a huge difference between books and experience. Where in the books did it say that her body would move on its own? That she would speak a mix of pleading babble and guttural moans?

That she would bite him on the shoulder?

Well, that might have been in the *Kama Sutra*.

She licked at the mark and felt him tremble. When he raised his head, she saw that he'd been laughing.

"Anji, I am so *glad* that you chose me for your husband," he told her. "And I must tell you something." His expression became very tender. "I love you, my wife. We've been married three days and have yet to spend a night together, but I would not wish to go through life without you."

"Nor I, you." Anji brushed his dark hair away from his forehead. "I knew you were my husband when you took my hand the day we met. But I knew I loved you when you gave me sleep as a gift."

He grinned. "Just so you know, there isn't going to be much sleep for you tonight."

"Just so you know, I had a long nap on the plane." Anji surprised him by pushing him onto his back and settling herself on top of him. "And that I believe in a modern marriage where the wife shoulders her share in the bedroom."

To demonstrate, Anji gave him a deep, openmouthed kiss, using her tongue in a suggestive rhythm.

Dev splayed his hands on her hips and thrust against her, matching the rhythm she set.

They'd banked their desire for so long, they could wait no

longer. Anji dragged her mouth away and rolled onto her back. Dev covered her body with his and settled between her legs, holding her face, kissing her and whispering a lot of nonsensical love words.

When Dev, with a gentle and exquisite slowness, joined them at last, Anji sobbed her relief before an explosive pleasure shook them both.

Afterward, they gazed into each other's eyes knowing they were joined together not only in this life, but all future lives.

1

UNINHIBITED

CARA BRANTLEY STARED at her reflection in the dressing-room mirror. This veil wasn't right, either. Why was it so hard to decide on a piece of tulle she'd wear on her head?

What was the matter with her?

She'd tried on dozens of bridal gowns. She'd tortured poor Elizabeth Gray, who had never indicated the slightest annoyance at spending hours and hours helping her into and out of dresses and putting up with Cara's mother and friends. So Cara had chosen a dress just to be done with it. An expensive dress. And it was a stunning dress. She looked good in it and at least Elizabeth would make a hefty profit and her relieved mother had let the poor videographer go home. But had she "known" it was "her" dress? No. She'd faked it.

Everyone, even Elizabeth, told her she would "know" when she put on the right one. Just the way they told her she'd know when it was true love.

Most of the time she thought she knew.

But not all the time.

People said her doubts were normal. They said it was the stress of the wedding. Marriage was a big step. Her life would change forever. Having a few qualms was not only normal, it was healthy.

So why couldn't she at least find the right veil?

She heard a burst of male laughter. Dallas and his grooms-men were getting fitted next door, which was why Cara was here today. Just in case there were questions.

Other than hers.

Ripping off the veil, Cara followed the laughter into the same fitting room where she had selected a wedding dress. Someone else's clothes were still hanging on the elegant ivory satin-padded hangers. Cara looked around, but didn't see a spare bride nearby. She was probably with the alterations seamstresses.

"Pink?" she heard through the wall. "Dal, you are so whipped."

"Why?" Cara's fiancé asked. "Pink doesn't bother me. I'm secure in *my* manhood, Tyrone."

There was another round of laughter.

"Pink looks good on you, Ty." That was Marcus, another of Dallas's fraternity brothers. "Makes your skin really 'pop.'"

Cara laughed along with the rest of them.

"I don't need my skin to do any 'popping.' I just wanna finish getting measured and get me some of that beer."

Ty's voice faded as he left the fitting room.

Hmm. That didn't sound good. On the other hand, was it really all that different from Cara and her bridesmaids drinking champagne?

Seconds later, Cara heard a howl that made her jump.

"This isn't the same color you're wearing!" Tyrone was back.

"I'm the groom," Dallas replied.

"What about the color he's wearing? That's no pansy-ass pink. You can barely tell it's pink."

"Austin is the best man."

Or was that the *better* man?

Cara crushed the tulle in her hands as Ty complained. Austin was the reason she was feeling so uncertain.

Dallas Varnell and his identical twin brother, Austin, were so different in personality, no one had trouble telling them apart.

People were drawn to Dallas. *She* was drawn to Dallas.

When she'd known both during college, he was the center of attention while his brother quietly sat and observed. Dallas's frequent efforts to include Austin had only emphasized their differences.

Austin was a downer, she'd heard people say back then, and she knew Austin had heard them say it, too. He was the responsible one, the designated driver, the rule follower and all those other mature qualities college guys didn't want to be reminded of.

"You act like an old man," Dallas complained to him once, when Austin had pointed out that he'd cut three calculus classes in a row. "No, you act like an old *woman!*"

Cara had been in their study group. That's how she'd met the Varnell twins. Dallas and his buddies had wanted to copy Austin's homework and Cara had told him not to let them.

In that instant, she'd captured the attention of *both* Dallas and Austin. Austin, because he thought he'd finally found someone who was immune to Dallas's charisma, and Dallas, because he thought the same thing.

He was so good-looking and outgoing that people didn't mind being manipulated by him because they enjoyed hanging around him. But for the first time, Dallas couldn't charm his way with a smile.

Austin was equally good-looking, but took exactly the opposite route. He was as reserved as Dallas was outgoing. He did favors; he didn't ask for them. He was responsible, dependable and studied hard, all excellent, but hardly sexy, qualities. Still, she'd liked him better.

Being with Austin had made Cara feel grown up. But it was such work to get to know him, and she'd discovered that he was contemptuous of anything he considered frivolous and unworthy of his time. He'd felt that way about a lot of things, things she enjoyed.

It was much easier to be with Dallas. And so for a time, she had been, even though she'd suspected he was only interested in her because his brother was. She'd actually hoped Austin might object, but he'd backed off, as he always did.

Eventually Cara moved on, and then last year, she'd crossed paths with the Varnell twins once again. Or at least Dallas.

Now working as a commercial interior designer, Cara was on-site with a client at the same time Dallas was making a sales call.

They caught up by meeting for coffee, which became drinks and dinner. She'd learned that Austin now worked for Wildcatter Investments, which amused her. Staid Austin had finally loosened up and it seemed that Dallas had tightened up—matured. Exactly what each had needed to do.

Cara had had fun. So when Dallas called her, she went out with him again. And again.

He worked in sponsorship sales for the Houston Texans football team, the perfect career for him. He entertained, gave away tickets and other perks and kept the money people happy. When they went out together, it was always to an event of some sort, always exciting and enjoyable and not something she could have experienced with anyone but an insider. It was thrilling. It was intoxicating. And soon, Cara only felt happiest when she was with Dallas.

The problem was that everyone felt that way, and she and Dallas were seldom alone.

The first time they slept together, it had been after an argument about that very thing. There had been tearful accusations (hers), promises (his) and ultimately the kind of make-up sex of legends.

And he'd proposed. Right then.

And she'd tearfully accepted. Right then.

And the cycle had repeated, except for the proposal.

When had she turned into a person who needed constant reassurance?

Cara didn't like this about herself. She and Dallas were older and he'd demonstrated his new maturity by making a commitment. He had a job where he worked long, erratic hours. She needed to get over herself.

However, there had been the question of a wedding date.

A fixed date proved as slippery as, well, something really slippery. They had to work around the team's game schedule. And then there were the playoffs and recruiting. Cara's winter wedding became a spring wedding, which meant different flowers and no velvet for the bridesmaids.

And now it was a summer wedding. With pink. Lots of pink. Pink that would look wrong in the fall, so this had better be the *last* time she rescheduled.

Dallas was so contrite. And she understood. Truly. And he'd make love to her with a skillful intensity that made her forgive him anything.

But.

They'd been engaged nearly a year and the wedding was still months away. Cara had allowed her mother to incorporate ever more complicated details to placate her about the delay.

And then there was the little matter of last month. Cara sank onto one of the padded white chairs in the fitting room. Her face heated and she knew she was blushing even though she was alone.

She'd been trying to talk to Dallas about the wedding and their future and just life in general. She was feeling emotionally disconnected and vulnerable and wanted to be with him. But he was busy and he didn't seem to understand her need for lengthy emotional exchanges.

They had a spectacular argument resulting in a spectacular nooner. Afterward, Cara had teased Dallas by saying that she was going to wait for him right there in his bed. Naked.

So when the front door opened shortly after he left, she assumed it was Dallas deciding that he didn't have to meet in person with whoever wanted to buy advertising for that week's game, and that he could just as easily work out the details over the telephone and stay in bed with her.

Naturally, she got out of bed to greet him. Naked.

And, understandably, she didn't realize immediately that the man in the foyer wasn't Dallas, but his twin, Austin, who watched as she merrily pranced down the stairs. Naked.

"I knew it, I knew it!" Laughing, she'd launched herself at him.

Just before her thighs clamped around his waist, her mind registered that she was intimately wrapped around a dark, navy blue suit instead of the casual sport coat Dallas had been wearing.

By then, it was too late to stop the kiss.

Warm hands supported her bare bottom as lips that were the same as Dal's acted so very differently.

They shouldn't have been acting at all.

And she shouldn't have been enjoying the performance.

Dal's kisses were perfect. Always. He knew what worked and nailed the moves every time. It was like watching a recorded performance versus live theater. One delivered guaranteed excellence. The other delivered the unexpected, sometimes good and sometimes bad.

And sometimes, perfection.

Cara's skin grew cold, then hot. Slowly she drew her head back and gazed at the man who just might have redefined perfection.

"Hello, Cara," Austin said.

2

_____

"Austin! I… Dallas and I are getting married!" she blurted out, although he almost certainly knew.

"Congratulations. Or is it best wishes to the bride?"

"What are you doing here?"

He smiled.

She hadn't seen Austin smile like that before. Then again, a naked woman had just flung herself into his arms and planted a wet one on him. He was entitled.

And about that… How was she supposed to extricate herself and get back up the stairs? She didn't have the guts to loosen her grip, turn around and nonchalantly walk back up the stairs knowing he was watching her. What a view. Not exactly her best. And running up the stairs with everything jiggling would just be pathetic.

"I'm picking up the tickets Dal left for me," Austin explained. "I have a key."

"Oh. He didn't mention that."

"He probably didn't think of it, since we do this all the time. He leaves tickets on the fireplace mantel and I stop by during lunch and pick them up. I'm setting you down now," he added in the same conversational tone.

Releasing her, he quickly shrugged out of his suit jacket and draped it over her shoulders.

Relief at his thoughtfulness made her knees shake. "Thank you."

"Thank *you*." And he grinned.

Austin Varnell *grinned*. He never grinned. Or he didn't used to. The old Austin would have awkwardly looked away. The old Austin wouldn't have kissed her that way. Or any way.

Clutching the jacket closed, Cara walked to the stairs quickly—but not in a way anyone could describe as a panicked retreat—and headed up the stairs, all jiggling safely hidden.

IN THE FITTING ROOM at Tuxedo Park, Austin was also reliving that day. He remembered every detail of the moments she'd spent in his arms. He remembered how her skin felt, her warmth, how she tasted, her lips, and especially the tiny sound she'd made when his tongue had met hers.

He remembered watching her climb the stairs until she was out of sight.

Cara Brantley, the love of his life.

And she was getting married to his brother.

She had no idea she was the love of his life, and neither did Dallas. Actually, Austin was stunned to discover it himself. All it had taken was her flinging herself naked into his arms and kissing him as though she couldn't let go.

Back when they were studying calculus together, he'd fantasized a really close scenario to what occurred that day. The surprise of it actually happening, years later, had exposed feelings he'd thought were gone.

No. Not gone. Hibernating. And now awake.

How very inconvenient.

Dallas hadn't stolen Cara away from him, or anything as dramatic as that. Dallas had gotten the girl simply by being himself.

Austin remembered the excruciating gatherings that neither he nor Cara had enjoyed. She'd been so much happier with Dallas. They'd suited each other then and obviously suited each other now.

Austin had been fine with that. At least he knew his future sister-in-law had a brain. Even better, she mitigated the worst of Dal's impulses because she recognized them and wasn't fooled by a wink and a smile. Cara was exactly who he needed.

But Cara was who Austin wanted.

He wouldn't have known if he hadn't stopped by for the tickets last month.

One look at Cara—and it had been a very long, naked look—and Austin had gone from being pleased at his brother's choice of wife to insanely covetous. He'd gone from feeling a brotherly fondness toward Cara to pure, but not so simple, lust.

Austin had only himself to blame. If there had been a single thing he'd learned with the Wildcatter team, it had been to go for it. Take risks. The only true failure was not making the attempt. And all the other motivational sayings that papered the offices.

Back in college, Austin should have pursued Cara instead of assuming that any woman who had a choice would choose Dallas. But he'd made no effort whatsoever because that way, he wouldn't get rejected. In effect, he'd rejected her first.

He should have accepted that Dal had a knack with women and he, Austin, would have to work at it more. It was just one of their differences, like Austin finding it easier to study than Dallas did.

But that was in the past.

After Cara had gone upstairs, Austin remembered walking over to the mantel, picking up the envelope holding the tickets and thinking that he needed to deal with his feelings for Cara, spend a few days wallowing in self-pity and then set those feelings aside. And he needed to accomplish this without climbing the stairs, knocking on the bedroom door and asking for closure sex.

Not a risk likely to result in a good return on investment.

He didn't climb the stairs. He opened the envelope, checked the dates on the tickets and grouped the consecutively numbered seats. He was aware when Cara came down the stairs but didn't look up.

"Here's your jacket," she said. "I appreciate your decency."

"No prob." Austin draped the jacket over his arm. "You're going to be my sister-in-law." *And I've seen you naked.*

"And you've seen me naked." She uncannily echoed his thoughts.

And the kiss? What about that hot, incredibly sexy kiss they'd shared? Maybe it hadn't been so incredible for her. "If you think about it, you've seen Dallas naked, so you know what I look like."

"Nice theory." She stepped closer to him and studied his face. "But you two don't look as much alike as you used to."

"Really?" He raised an eyebrow and she gave him a chastising look.

"From a distance, sure, you look alike, and certainly to those who don't know you well."

"Then what's different?"

"Your eyes most of all. Dal has crinkles around his from smiling so much. He's been in the sun more and it shows. I try to get him to wear sunscreen, but he forgets."

"He doesn't like the smell."

"Who does? Now you, you've got a tiny little frown line between your eyebrows."

He rubbed at it before he could stop himself.

"Also, now that I've seen you, I have to say that all the salty party snacks and the irregular eating and sleeping schedule are beginning to catch up with Dal."

She was talking about his twin. He shouldn't feel so smug.

"Anyway." Cara crossed her arms and stared at her shoes. "I'm completely mortified by what happened. I know that someday Dal and I will laugh about it."

"But not yet."

"No."

He liked that she assumed he knew when to be discreet without begging him not to tell Dallas. "How about us? Are we ever going to laugh about it?"

She looked up at him. "We are never going to talk about it again."

"No." But that didn't mean he wasn't going to think about the way she'd felt in his arms and the fact that she'd kissed him back. *She'd kissed him back.* And at that point, she must have known she wasn't kissing Dallas.

She'd kissed *him* back.

"We will act as though it never happened."

She'd kissed him back. "If you wish."

"I wish."

He tapped the ticket envelope against his palm. "In that case, see you around, Cara."

SHE'D KISSED HIM. She'd known it was Austin and not Dallas as soon as their lips touched, but she'd kissed him anyway. It was time to acknowledge it.

For weeks, Cara had convinced herself that, because it was so uncharacteristic of Austin to take advantage, she'd been surprised into immobility.

Immobile if she didn't count her lips. They sure hadn't been immobile.

As long as she put the incident out of her mind and didn't think about it, she might not remember her tongue finding its way into his mouth. And…there might have been the tiniest little moan on her part, but the thought was too horrible to contemplate.

Cara propped her elbows on her knees and covered her face with her palms. All around her were the sounds of happy brides choosing their wedding gowns, plastic bags dragging across the carpet and, from the fitting room on the other side, a couple of bridesmaids whining about their dresses.

Here in the dressing room at the end, Cara had found an oasis of calm. She could just sit and breathe, at least until the bride whose dressing room this was returned.

Unfortunately, along with the sitting and breathing came the thinking. And what she was thinking about was this: if she truly loved Dallas, how could she so enjoy kissing Austin?

She *thought* she loved Dallas; she wouldn't have agreed to marry him otherwise. She loved being with him. She loved the way he made her feel in and out of bed. She missed him when he wasn't with her. Life was brighter and better with him.

But.

Did *she* make his life brighter and better? What did she bring to the table? Why had Dallas proposed to *her,* Cara?

Why didn't she know?

Anytime she protested that they never spent much time alone, they usually ended up in bed. Afterward, when they lay cocooned in each other's arms, Cara could hear a faint sound that she knew was his cell phone vibrating against whatever counter he'd left it on as messages, e-mails and texts streamed in.

He could tune it out, but she couldn't, and the buzz always triggered a low-level anxiety that she didn't understand. It was his job. He was busy. She put out her fair share of fires from suppliers, contractors and clients at all hours, too.

The longer their engagement, the more Cara felt as though she was fighting for any little piece of Dallas she could get.

She'd tell him how she felt, she decided. And she'd make him discuss it with her and not cajole her into thinking she was being clingy and insecure.

Ugh. She sat up. She *was* being clingy and insecure. She hated clingy women. Lately, all she ever did was complain and criticize him or bring up wedding details. Maybe if she weren't such a Debbie Downer, he'd stick around longer. And if she were more fun to be around, he'd seek *her* out for a change.

The revelation was so simple, it was embarrassing. This was boy-girl 101.

Someone came into the men's fitting room. She heard rustling and then the sound of a zipper being zipped or unzipped.

"Hey, Dal?" she heard. "Where are you? The guy out there wants to know what color of white shirt we're supposed to wear. Oh, hey." The voice had arrived at the door of the dressing room. "Do you know what color shirt we're supposed to wear?"

"White?" Dal answered.

"Man, they got five different colors of white. There's diamond white and eggshell and candle something and a couple more."

"I have no idea," Dal said.

Not surprising since Cara hadn't even known about the white choices.

"Just get measured and we'll ask Cara later."

"Gotcha." She heard whoever it was slap the side of the door and leave.

Listening a few moments more, she decided that Dal was alone.

She leaned against the wall. "Hey, sailor. Lookin' for a good time?"

"Cara?"

"If that's what you want to call me," she answered suggestively.

"What are you doing?" There was uncertain laughter in his voice.

Good. She wanted to keep him surprised. "I got me an itch and I'm lookin' to get it scratched." It was a miracle she didn't crack up.

"I've heard they have creams for that."

Cara pressed her lips together until she could control her voice. "Oooh, creams. I love creams. They're so…creamy." She made a face in the mirror. Come on. She could do better than that. "I love spreading them all over my skin. And I do mean *all* over. They leave everything nice and slick."

"I thought creams just softened."

Cara rolled her eyes. *Get with the program, already!*

"For slick, nothing beats oil," he said.

"Really?" she prompted. "Tell me why." And if he answered "higher viscosity," she was going to give up.

"You can get much longer strokes."

That might be sexy. Unless he was discussing car pistons or something. He needed to work the voice a little more, though. Maybe he was worried about his buddies hearing him. "Ooooh," she said, mostly to fill the silence. "Would you like to stroke me?" Honestly, she sounded like a bad Marilyn Monroe impersonator.

"Yes."

Ah. His voice had warmed up. "Tell me *all* about it."

She heard him move and guessed he'd sat down.

"You're lying naked on the bed."

"Well, of course."

"On your stomach. I pour oil on my palms and rub them together to warm it."

Cara leaned her head back, imagining Dal doing the same on his side. "What does it smell like?"

"Oil."

She smiled, waiting.

"Scented with…musk. But not the cheap hippie musk. The good stuff."

Cara rolled her eyes. Dal obviously did better in front of an audience where he could gauge their reaction. An interesting insight. "The stuff that smells like sex," she said because she just thought of it.

"Oh, yeah. That would be the stuff."

"So your hands are all slick and slippery. What are you going to do with them?"

As she spoke, Cara noticed that several veils were clipped to hangers on one of the hooks above her. Surely the other bride wouldn't mind if she just took a look at them.

She reached for one when Dal began to speak.

"I'm going to start at the small of your back and move my thumbs over the base of your spine right on the spot that gets tight when you sit for too long."

Cara blinked. That was pretty specific. He must be getting into this. She started to reply, but he continued without prompting.

"I'm going to rub harder and faster so the warmth will melt all the knots. When, and only when I hear you purr, I'll pour a tiny pool of oil into the hollow of your back."

Purr? Cara didn't remember ever purring. Dal had never given her a massage like that, though.

"Then I'll smear the oil around at your waist and stroke all the way up to your shoulders."

"A very long stroke." Cara saw a chapel-length veil that was only a single layer of tulle and completely unadorned. Her dress was so heavily beaded that an elaborate veil would fight with it. Maybe that was what the problem had been.

She unclipped it from the hanger.

"Many long strokes. As your muscles relax and warm, I'll press deeper and slower. I'll enjoy the feel of your warm, slick skin beneath my fingers. You'll stretch and sigh. I'll pour oil on your shoulders and work out the kinks and knots."

"That feels wonderful." Cara realized she'd been staring at the veil without really seeing it. She could deal with veils later. "Don't stop."

"I'm just getting started. Now I pour a different oil into my palm. This one warms and sensitizes. It might tingle. Are there places you want to tingle?"

"Oooh." Marilyn again. "Some places are already tingling." And it wasn't a lie.

"What places?"

"Neglected places."

"Tell me."

He'd lobbed back to her. All right then. "Here's poor little me, lying on the bed all naked and you've completely ignored my rump. So I arch my back and give a little wiggle to attract your attention."

"And it works. I look down your back and see two globes just begging for me to touch them."

Globes? He said globes?

"And I do, spreading my fingers and the oil all over. All. Over. But this is the oil that heats and you aren't expecting that. You gasp and raise yourself to look over your shoulder at me. You're so beautiful. Your back glistens. Your hair falls over one shoulder and you're unaware that you've revealed the side of your breast."

Her eyes widened as he painted the image in her mind.

"You see my hands on your bottom, kneading and heating. The tingling begins and you stare into my eyes. You know what you want and I know it, too."

Cara dropped the veil.

It broke the trance Dal's words had put her in, which was a good thing. Once he'd caught on, he'd *caught on.* Her heart was going like gangbusters and she'd been taking quick, shallow breaths.

"But you can't have what you want until you ask for it," he continued, his voice rough. "And you want it. You're desperate for it."

"Yes!"

"Ask me, Cara. Ask me for what you want."

"I want to know why you love me." She hadn't been going to say that at all. But it was what she truly wanted. "Tell me. Please."

There was silence. Yeah, she was changing gears from fantasy to reality, but maybe they'd created a mood that would make it easier for Dal to tap into his deeper emotions.

Cara held her breath. She was asking for more than his usual "I love you, babe." Or "You know I'm crazy about you." Or even, "You're the best thing that's ever happened to me."

Why? Why was she the best thing that had ever happened to him? Specifics, she wanted specifics.

And then he spoke. "You complete me."

Cara nearly screamed. She'd wanted deep emotion and he'd given her a movie cliché? "That's been said. A lot."

"But it's true."

Cara wanted to cry. Actually, she wanted *not* to cry, but figured it was inevitable. "I—I was hoping for more."

And then the words poured out of him. "You not only make me want to be a better man, you make me understand why I need to be a better man. I want to be worthy of you, of being your life partner. I want to be your strength when you need it and your support when you don't. I want to hold you when you need holding and I want to be held when I feel weak. And I want to know that I can depend on you to get my back and be there even if I fail. I want to know that no matter how bad the day was, you'll be there when I come home at night. And I want to do the same for you. And to do that, I have to be the best man I can be. Cara, meeting you expanded my world. I see life not just through my eyes, but yours, too. I think more. I think differently. I feel more. I *am* more."

Now the tears were okay. This was the connection she'd been missing. The lack had been the source of her unease. She simply needed to bond on a deeper level than Dallas did. Like most men, he'd assumed she knew how he felt. He didn't have to talk it to death. He probably hadn't analyzed it until now. He just knew the feelings were there and that was enough. For pity's sake, he was marrying her. What more proof did she need?

Cara smiled through her tears as she imagined him thinking exactly that to himself. "Thank you for telling me. I needed to hear that."

His voice was so quiet she almost missed his next words. "I needed to say it. I love you, Cara. I always will."

"Hello?" Someone knocked on the door before opening it. "Is anyone… Oh, good. You're still here." Lia, the assistant manager, stood in the doorway. "They had a question about the shirts next door. It'll just take a second."

Cara quickly dabbed at her eyes.

"Having a meltdown?" Lia smiled sympathetically. "Don't worry. Sooner or later every bride has one. It only means you need a break. Come with me."

Rather than explain, Cara followed her.

"We've got peach iced tea brewed today. I'm going to get you a glass. You can relax in a comfy chair and if you're up to it, pick which shade of white you want the groomsmen to wear. If you're not up to it, I can pick."

"I can't believe it matters that much," Cara said. Not compared to having just heard her fiancé's deepest feelings.

It had been the most emotionally moving moment of her life. Who cared about shades of white?

"It's mostly for the photos." Lia chattered away. "We find that when a bride wears an off-white dress, or has a lot of embellishment that makes it appear off-white from a distance, white shirts will make the dress look dirty. They also seem to skew the rest of the colors."

"Oh."

"It's an easy fix." They emerged into the main salon. "And this very helpful gentleman brought all five shirts over so you can hold them up to your dress and pick the one you like."

"Hey, babe," said a grinning Dallas.

3

DALLAS FANNED OUT the five packaged shirts like a hand of cards and offered them to Cara. "Pick one."

No. Nonononono. "I— You do it," she said to Lia. "I trust your judgment."

Because she no longer trusted her own.

As Lia took the shirts from Dallas, and, yes, there was no doubt that it was Dallas who stood before her, Cara tried to calculate how he could have uttered those beautiful words, grabbed five shirt samples and run from the fitting room next door in time to be standing in the salon here when Cara walked out of the dressing room. And not be breathing hard.

It must be possible because…because otherwise, she'd just been talking smutty with Austin.

Which was not something her mind was going to accept.

"Dal?"

He held up a finger as he read a text message, then snapped the phone closed and smiled. "What's up?"

"Do I complete you?"

"What?" He laughed. "Did you see *Jerry Maguire* on cable last night or something?"

"Do I *complete* you?"

Dal took a step backward. "Do you think I need completing?"

"Don't you?"

He shook his head. "See, I don't think a guy should look for someone else to provide what's missing in his life. He should already be a whole person."

Good point. Excellent point. Perfectly acceptable point. "So you don't *need* me."

He took her hand and brushed his thumb across her knuckles. "Not need, *want*."

"Why?"

Irritation flashed across his face. "Babe, do we have to discuss this now?" He lowered his voice. "We could go somewhere private, maybe get a hotel room. Yeah. Let's do that." He smiled his most winsome smile. "Instead of telling you how much I want you, I'll show you."

As usual. "You just want to use sex to distract me."

He looked up at her from beneath raised eyebrows. His signature look. "Is it working?"

"Not this time."

His expression abruptly changing from coaxing to frustration, Dallas dropped her hand. "I don't know what you want from me, Cara!"

You can't have what you want until you ask for it. "I want to know why you love me."

"Not this again," she heard him mutter under his breath. "Look, you're great for me. Right from the very beginning— and I'm talking back in school—you saw me. Like in *The Wizard of Oz* when they see behind the curtain. When everybody else is looking at the smoke and mirrors, you see me behind the curtain." He quirked a smile at her. "And you love me anyway."

"I do." Cara felt a rush of affection for him. She'd just have to accept that talking about deep emotions wasn't his style. "You want to go to lunch with the guys, don't you?"

"Yeah, we thought we'd check out the microbrewery where they get the beer next door." He tilted his head. "Are we okay?"

"We will be."

However, his twin might not be.

After Dallas left, Cara went back to the dressing room, fully expecting to find it occupied. Surprised that it wasn't on such a busy day, she entered and knocked once on the wall. "You still there, sailor?"

"Aye, aye, Cap'n."

She'd aye-aye *him*. So he'd waited at the scene of the crime. "You know, I was thinking…we hardly spend any time alone." Wasn't *that* the truth. "Let's stay in Rocky Falls tonight. I have to meet with the florist at one o'clock, and the photographer wants us to check out the park. Why don't you book the room and I'll get us a romantic picnic supper."

There was a telling silence. "That's not a good idea."

"It's a wonderful idea! It'll save us an extra trip up here."

"I can't tonight. I've got a full schedule."

"That's what you always say!" Cara added a loud sniff. "If…if I'm important to you at all, meet me at the gazebo at five-thirty."

AUSTIN CLOSED his eyes. All he'd wanted was the memory, something to keep for himself. And knowing that he'd told her he loved her. Cara was going to marry Dallas, and Austin had to live with that for a very long time. She'd shown him what an arrogant ass he'd been. And he believed her because she was the only woman he'd ever known who saw right through his brother. Now, it was time for damage control.

ALL AFTERNOON, Cara expected to get a phone call from Austin telling her that Dallas was sorry, but he couldn't make it. If Austin was really desperate, he'd borrow Dallas's cell phone so his number would show on Cara's caller ID and cancel that way.

If…if I'm important to you at all, meet me at the gazebo at five-thirty. She'd never issue a juvenile ultimatum like that. She'd just wanted Austin to squirm. In a bad way, not a good way.

Cara had several very different reactions to learning that

she'd been talking to Austin. Oddly, embarrassment wasn't one of them. She'd thought she was having a little sexy fun with the man she was going to marry—nothing to be embarrassed about.

Austin had known it, too. And that was unforgivable. It had gone way beyond a joke. Deceiving her that way wasn't in Austin's character. So why had he done it? If he actually showed up at the gazebo, she was going to ask him.

What she'd do with the answer, she had no idea.

After she and the florist had discussed flowers, they walked over to the Rocky Falls Community Church to assess the space. The florist had been wildly enthusiastic about the Chrysanthemum Wedding, as it was now called. All shades of pink ranging from the very lightest next to the bride and groom, to the deepest rose on the outside of the aisles, would be echoed in the floral choices.

Hadn't anyone ever thought of it before? Cara was an interior designer—she knew about making a dramatic impact and focal points and using color. She also knew how easy it was to get carried away at the expense of the budget. She was lucky her parents wanted to pay for most of the wedding. But that wasn't why she'd stayed behind at the church after the florist left.

It was a contemporary church with sleek lines, blond wood and natural stone. The silence made it a good place to think, which was why Cara was sitting here.

When she'd thought she'd made the deeper emotional connection with Dallas, she had felt such relief to have identified the source of her "something's not right" feeling. Only, it turned out she hadn't connected with Dallas. She hadn't connected with Austin, either. It was all just a fake.

She still needed that deeper, emotional connection, the feeling she was sharing her soul with someone who felt that way, too. Dallas didn't need that. He loved her and that was enough for him.

Why wasn't it enough for her? Why couldn't she accept that

they had different love styles? Maybe hers was a female style and his was a male style. She might have believed all couples were like that if Austin hadn't told her why he supposedly loved her. He had been sharing his soul.

Whether he meant it or not wasn't the issue—for now anyway. Solving the problem he'd unerringly illustrated was the issue.

Cara reached into her purse for the notebook she kept with her always. She'd identified the problem, now she'd list solutions.

She could continue trying to connect with Dallas, maybe get him into some couples' therapy. Except that Dallas would easily learn to say the right words and charm the therapist.

So, if he never tapped into his deeper emotions, she could accept what they had, which was pretty darn good, or walk away and hope she could find that connection with someone else, someone not named Varnell.

She was like a game-show contestant who had to bet a perfectly good prize for a chance to see what was behind door number two.

It was late afternoon, and she needed to get on the road back to Houston. It was tempting to drive on out of town, but she swung by the park first in case Austin actually showed up.

She turned off the ignition, and from the parking lot, she could see a man standing in the gazebo.

Slamming the car door, Cara started down the narrow asphalt path toward the gazebo. She had no idea what to say to him, so she was just going to wing it.

"Hey, there you are!" He bounded down the steps and met her on the path. "This place is great. We're going to get some awesome pix."

Dallas smiled down at her and leaned in for a kiss.

Dallas. This was not one of the possibilities she'd considered.

"Hey, where's the food? I thought we could walk over to the falls and eat there."

"The last I heard, you were too busy, so I didn't expect to see you." Cara wondered how he was going to play this.

Dallas draped an arm around her waist. "I knew how important this was to you, babe."

They began walking on the paved path that would lead them to the falls. The falls weren't high or dramatic, just unexpected in this area of Texas, and remarkably pretty.

Their rushing sound camouflaged Cara's silence, but not the buzzing of Dallas's cell phone.

"What's up?" He listened and said, "Nah. Don't worry about it," before flipping the phone shut. "Bad news on the hotel room. There's some festival going on in New Braunfels and rooms are booked solid everywhere. Austin found a motel, but said it looked hinky."

"That's okay. It was a spur-of-the-moment idea."

They'd reached the first of many "scenic photo opportunities" and sat on one of the wooden benches, a thoughtful gift from Mr. and Mrs. Julian Wainright, according to the tasteful brass plaque.

They stared at the falls. "You had something planned tonight, didn't you?" she asked.

"No big deal." His mouth tilted up. "Austin is going to cover for me. At least he's going to try."

"What was it?"

"Oh—" he shrugged it off "—sponsors' party in the owner's box at the stadium. Austin has been there before, so he knows the layout."

"And if people mistake him for you, so much the better."

"Yeah, but he'd be doing it even if he weren't my twin."

"Because you're covering for him," Cara said.

The falls splashed in the background. Dallas looked at her carefully. She could see him trying to figure out what she knew and what she didn't know.

"The only reason you're here is because Austin talked to you and told you what happened."

Dallas didn't say anything.

"I didn't know I was talking to him until you brought the shirts and I figured out you couldn't be in two places at once."

"No," he admitted.

"You were trying to protect my feelings."

Dallas shifted on the bench and raised his eyebrows. "From what he told me, I figured that was the way to go."

Cara felt a rush of affection. "You know what, Dallas? I don't think I've ever loved you more than I do right at this very moment."

"For real?"

She nodded. "What you're doing shows great sensitivity. You put my feelings ahead of an important gathering of moneymen. Why, this must be the sponsorship kickoff."

Dallas shifted again. His heel began to bounce up and down.

Cara continued, "The whole football season could be impacted by the tone of this party. You need to have someone who can make sure things are hopping and the mood is exciting and that everyone believes the team is headed for the playoffs."

Dallas glanced at her and then away. He twisted the heavy class ring he wore.

"But you jeopardized all that—and you did, because we both know Austin will be way out of his element. You jeopardized all that to put me first."

"It was Austin's idea," he muttered.

And that was why Dallas wasn't right for her. Cara took pity on him. "I know. But you went along with it and I'll never forget that."

"Yeah, well." Both feet were tapping now and he stared at his hands.

"Dallas."

He looked at her.

"Why did you ask me to marry you that night? We'd never discussed marriage."

He blew out his breath. "You were so unhappy. I wanted you to be happy. You're good for me. And I'm good for you, right?"

"Yes." But there needed to be so much more.

"And I love you. I do, Cara."

She looked into his handsome face. He meant it. He truly did. "But you're not *in* love with me."

"Love, in love, it's the same thing."

"No, it's not." She smiled and kissed his cheek. "I need someone who's in love with me." She pulled off her engagement ring and handed it to him. "Someday when you know the difference, you'll thank me."

He stared at the ring. "You're breaking up with me?"

"I'm not thrilled about it. But here's what would happen. I would keep bugging you about telling me how you feel and you would resent it. We'd argue. I'd be unhappy and you would start avoiding me. And then I'd nag you about that. In a few years, we'd hate each other."

"Gee, Cara." Dallas took the ring. As he twisted it in his fingers, the diamond caught the afternoon light. "Are you *in* love with Austin?" He sounded bitter and Cara had never heard that before.

"No." She shook her head. "No, no and no."

"But you're attracted to him."

"He's your identical twin. Clearly, he's my type. Now hurry up and call him so you can get to the party."

Dallas pressed his forehead to hers. "I would have married you."

"I know."

"I don't understand why my love wasn't enough."

"I know that, too. But you will find someone and you will fall in love with her and then you'll understand. And when you do, you call me and say, 'Now I get it.' Okay?"

"Deal." Leaning back, he grinned his patented Dallas grin. "Until then…friends with benefits?"

"No!"

Laughing, Dallas flipped open his phone. "Dude, we're busted.

Get back here and pick me up." As he closed the phone, he checked his watch. "He's already thirty minutes down the road."

Cara dug in her purse. "Take my car." She handed him the keys. "Austin can drive me back."

Dallas jingled the keys as he gave her a measuring look. "Do me a favor and don't cancel the wedding until you talk with Austin."

The wedding. Her mother. Ugh.

"Just a few adjustments to the guest list and a couple of new groomsmen and you're good to go."

"Dal!"

"I'm just sayin'."

4

He wasn't sorry.

Austin walked toward the bench where Cara sat staring at the falls. No matter how bad this conversation got, he wasn't sorry for telling her how he felt.

And he wasn't sorry for the sexy talk, either. Sure, he wished he could have prevented her from feeling embarrassed. He regretted wronging his brother, which he'd actually been trying to avoid. Rather than let his feelings boil away inside and perhaps explode in the future, he'd sought to release them safely.

To be honest, he was only sorry he'd been caught. That's right, Austin Varnell, straightest of straight arrows, had been a naughty boy.

So sue him.

That probably wasn't the best attitude to take into a conversation with his future sister-in-law.

Truly, he was only a rebel in his mind. He would do the gentlemanly thing and deliver a groveling apology with repeated assurances that he Didn't Think of Her That Way.

In other words, he would lie, because how could he not think of her that way? She'd run toward him naked, flung herself into his arms and kissed him. He didn't have to imagine what she looked like—he knew. So when he'd described massaging her with oils, he could visualize her body perfectly. And had. And would for a very long time.

And he was about to tell her he wouldn't. Right.

Austin wasn't good at lying, but he was good at keeping his feelings hidden. Sometimes.

Cara had noticed him and was watching as he approached the bench.

She was so…so Cara. The Cara who had made him realize that he'd had a little superiority thing going on. That he'd mistakenly believed that people who laughed and talked about nothing were shallow and not worth their time. Cara had taught him that socializing had value. He'd never be a natural at it like Dal, but he was no longer the supercilious lump on the sofa, either.

But what had he given to her? Nothing good.

Austin reached the bench, opened his mouth to deliver the apology that would allow them to meet at future family gatherings with a minimum of awkwardness—and told her, "I'm not sorry. And I meant every word I said. Every. Single. Word." Then he sat down.

He'd never been good at lying.

"Is that supposed to make me feel better? Because it doesn't."

"I feel better."

"This isn't about you." She gave him a withering look and stared out at the falls. "Why did you let me think you were Dallas?"

"Because it was the only chance I would ever have to talk to you as a lover. I could tell you how I felt and you'd never know. So I went for it."

"I'd never know?" She looked at him in disbelief. "You didn't think there'd be a conversation like, 'Oooh, Dal, let's do the massage thing.' 'What massage thing?' 'You know, with the special oil? The one we fantasized about in the dressing room that day?' You didn't think there'd ever be a conversation like that?" She threw her hands up in the air.

"Dal's next line would have been 'I don't remember—why don't you remind me.' And then neither of you would have cared," Austin said.

He thought he saw a flicker of a smile before she turned away. "You've ruined massages for me."

"I can fix that."

"Stop it," she said coldly. "Flirting with your brother's fiancée is completely out of line."

Except while she'd been flinging her hands around, Austin had noticed something. He reached for her left hand and rubbed his thumb over her bare ring finger. "Are you still my brother's fiancée?" Dal hadn't said anything, but Dal was mad at him right now and justifiably so.

Cara snatched her hand away and crossed her arms. "No."

Austin's heart began beating in heavy thuds. "Then I'm not out of line."

"You think you can just move right in? One brother is as good as another? Maybe I won't notice the difference? You two are *nothing* alike! Dal would never sneak around behind your back and do what you did. He genuinely loved me—in his comfortable, easy-breezy way. He has no idea that love can be so…" She gestured as she sought the words. "Intense. Rich. Deep." She dropped her hands. "More."

Austin knew. "You mean the kind of love where you would rather suffocate than breathe the air of a world without your beloved? The kind of love that burns so hot it frightens you and you back away from it because you're afraid you'll get hurt? You bury it and think you've put it out. But one day, a naked woman flings herself into your arms and knocks away the ash. And you realize the fire was only banked and now it's burning hotter than ever."

Cara had slowly turned her head until she was looking straight at him. Straight into his eyes.

"But it's too late," he continued. "So you say what you should have said before and hope it's enough to bank the fire again. Because you know the fire will never completely go out."

They stared at each other. "Is that the love you're talking about?" he asked her.

Cara looked dazed. "Yeah. That's it."

"That's how I feel. It's how I've always felt."

"Then why didn't you tell me?"

"Look what happened when I did." He waited a beat and then asked, "Are you still mad at me?"

"Yes!"

He nodded thoughtfully. "You're mad at me, Dal is mad at me, the engagement is off…so I don't have anything to lose by kissing you."

Quickly grasping either side of her face, Austin kissed her the best going-for-broke, all-in, bet-the-farm, one-shot kiss of his life…and won his heart's desire.

Three months later

"ALL RIGHT, GENTLEMEN." Cara heard the wedding coordinator talking in the room next to the bride's parlor at the Rocky Falls Community Church. "We're ready for you to line up— not you, Mr. Varnell. We don't want you to accidentally see the bride."

Cara waited until the groomsmen shuffled out and tapped on the wall. "Hey, sailor. Whatcha wearin'?"

"Cara?"

She laughed. "Yes. Austin?"

"Absolutely."

"What's the code?"

"Cara…"

"Come on."

"I burn for you," he said in a low voice.

"Oooh. That makes me hot," she said.

"Cara, what are you doing?"

"Just fanning the flames."

"In the *church?*"

Such an Austin response. She loved, *loved* poking through his layer of reserve to the passionate man beneath. "It'll give you something to think about during the ceremony."

He was the one. She knew it, just as everyone had told her she would. Hokey as it sounded, she felt they were soul mates.

If she ever doubted her decision to break up with Dallas, she had only to remember how quickly her love had become affection. When Dal found the right woman, he was going to be stunned at the difference.

"So," she prompted Austin. "Tell me what you're wearing."

Reluctantly, he quickly recited what he was wearing, ending with, "and a vest and cravat in Bridal Blush pink."

"And?"

"Is there supposed to be anything else?"

"You tell me. Are you wrapping your package? Or are you leaving it unwrapped so it'll be easier to sneak away and exchange presents during the reception?"

"Cara!" He strangled her name.

Good.

Since that evening at the falls, Austin had determinedly wooed her. And she had determinedly resisted.

Until Dallas had called her. "Would you give the guy a break? You want emotion? He's emoting all over the place. I can't take it anymore."

So Cara had relented. She'd never gotten around to canceling the wedding, anyway.

But she invoked a no-sex rule. Not to punish Austin, but to make sure she wasn't distracted by sex before she knew that they had a true emotional connection.

Like *that* had been a problem.

So the sex ban had become a game of holdout. Who would crack first? Who would beg the other?

There would be only winners in this game.

Austin cleared his throat. "I'll unwrap my present if you'll unwrap yours."

"Don't be silly!" Cara laughed. "I never wrapped mine."

She heard the breath hiss between his teeth just as the wedding coordinator entered the room. Ha. Perfect timing.

"Are you ready, Cara?" she asked.

"I am *so* ready."

IT HAD TO HAVE BEEN the longest ceremony in the history of weddings.

Then there had been the ten million photographs because all kinds of people wanted a picture of their Chrysanthemum Wedding. Right now, Austin hated chrysanthemums. And wedding photographers.

"You're being so patient," Cara cooed at him.

They were being arranged in yet another pose, this time on the top steps with the rest of the wedding party below them. "I am not."

"Are you thinking about my present?"

He looked down at her. Deliberately he moved his hand and squeezed her bottom through the beaded dress.

"So you are!"

Her impish laughter faded as Austin continued to knead and caress her. "They have enough pictures," he said.

"They have enough pictures." She sighed.

And that was it. Austin had reached his breaking point. For the past three months, he'd waited. He'd given her time and space, though not a lot of time and only a little space. He'd respected her boundaries and even understood her reasoning. He didn't like it, but he understood it.

He'd proposed after a week.

She'd turned him down.

So he'd proposed after two weeks.

And she'd turned him down.

The next day, he'd arrived on her doorstep with a basket of massage oils and massaged just her hands. He pretended each finger was a different part of her body and demonstrated what he planned to do with that body part when he had the chance.

The day after that, Cara proposed to *him*.

Now, Austin took her hand and led her through the chrysanthemum petals and down the aisle.

No one stopped them.

Cara's mother hurried after them. "Stop looking at each other like that!" she instructed through a clenched smile. "People are talking. Remember the video. Stand up straight, Cara. Make sure you hold the bouquet— Wait! Where are you going?"

"To give Austin his present." She smiled up at him and he felt his knees buckle.

"Oh. Now? Should I send the videographer with you?"

"No," they both answered.

"But—"

"See you at the reception!" Cara called as Austin helped her into the limousine.

It was a short, tense drive to the Wainright Inn and a shorter, tenser elevator ride up to the bridal suite. There was no way Austin was going to touch his bride. If he did so, he would abandon all civilized behavior. He glanced at her. She wore a smug expression.

Smug? She was smug and he was desperate. "You planned this."

"Oh, yeah."

"You truly wanted me insane with lust during our *wedding?*"

She leaned up against him and licked his ear. "You betcha."

"That tells me you've never driven a man insane with lust before. It's not slow and tender and pretty. It's raw and elemental and…goal oriented." He was sweating.

"Promise?" she asked in a provocative voice.

They literally ran off the elevator. Austin swiped the key

card, drew her inside and had her pressed up against the wall in a deep kiss before the door latched.

"Ow!"

She was lucky he heard her, being insane with lust as he was.

"What?" he panted.

"My veil. It's smashed up against the wall and all the pins are stabbing me in the head!"

"Take it off."

"I can't! My hair—I'll never get it pinned back up!"

"Does it have to be pinned up?"

"Yes!"

Austin pulled her into the living room. "I'll be careful. No running my fingers through your hair." He kissed her throat, urgently moving to the bodice of her strapless gown where her breasts swelled demurely.

He didn't want demure. He wanted flesh in his hands. He wanted nipples in his mouth. His fingers brushed the edge of her dress and he met resistance.

He pushed. "Is this glued to you or something?"

"Taped," she answered breathlessly. "So it won't slip."

Austin stared at her. "But…how do I get to you?"

"You sit on the bed." Cara kissed him, walking him backward as she did so. "And you get out your present."

His present nearly burst through the zipper. As Austin dropped his pants and sat on the bed, Cara stood in front of him and shimmied the beaded sheath over her hips, bunching it at her waist.

Austin went dry-mouthed as she revealed white lace-edged stockings hooked to long garters that were attached to a lacy thing just below her waist. Austin didn't care about the lacy thing. He barely noticed the lacy thing. What he did notice was that there was nothing below the lacy thing except Cara's dark blond curls.

Best. Present. Ever.

She straddled him and Austin had to consciously remind himself to breathe. She started to lower herself and he said, "Wait."

Running his hands up the backs of her thighs, past the lace-topped stockings, he gripped her bare buttocks. "I need to do this," he murmured.

Bringing her to his mouth, he gave her the most intimate of kisses.

"Auuusstinnn…" Cara moaned and clutched his shoulders as he used his tongue to excite her, learning her scent, her taste and the places that made her gasp and squirm. He laved her with a rhythm that had her gasping and rocking against him.

And then, "Austin—stop."

Not the words he'd expected to hear. In fact, hadn't she meant to say, "Don't stop?"

"Please." She tugged at his hair. "Trust me, this will be the only time I ever stop you, but I want our first time to be together."

"Okay." He should have been more eloquent, but that was all he had.

Gazing into his eyes, she lowered her body onto his, sheathing him within her warmth. Austin's eyes were squeezed shut so tightly he saw purple spots. He'd waited so long. He'd wanted so long.

"Don't move or I'll explode," Austin whispered, and opened his eyes to find her looking at him with a tender expression.

They sat, joined together, and smiled at each other. "What are you thinking?" Cara asked dreamily.

She expected him to think? "Um, something incredibly romantic."

"What?"

Afterward, he'd teach her not to ask complicated questions when they were in the throes of passion.

"I'm thinking that my bride didn't wear panties on her wedding day." He grinned. "I find that incredibly romantic."

"Austin, that's not what I meant."

He thrust upward, making her gasp and effectively distracting her.

Wearing a wicked grin, she returned the favor.

Austin took over, guiding her hips in a quick rhythm that had them both shuddering their climaxes within moments.

"Wow." Cara looked shocked. "That was fast."

Austin exhaled. "I needed that. I so needed that." Resting his head on her shoulder, he added, "I may live now."

"Hmm." Cara stretched her arms over her head. "I feel much more relaxed."

Austin nuzzled her throat. "I've been practicing my massage techniques. Want to skip the reception?"

"They'd come find us. My mother would get the manager to unlock the door."

"Any manager would know better than to unlock the bridal suite when the bride and groom might be inside."

"We don't have time, anyway." Cara shifted and then raised an eyebrow at Austin. "Really? Already?"

He smiled. "The fire blazes anew."

"That's some fire." And Cara began a slow, rhythmic rocking.

"It's not about the fire, Cara. It's about the love that fuels the fire."

She gripped him and moved faster.

"Well, maybe a little about the fire."

THE RECEPTION WAS UNDER WAY when Cara and Austin slipped into the ballroom at the Wainright Inn.

"Oh, look. She's just glowing," a guest commented to Mrs. Brantley. "What is that shade of pink?"

Mrs. Brantley smiled tightly. "Bridal Blush."

1

UNBRIDALED

GINA WELLS SURVEYED the wine list at Lily's on Lakeway, one of the finest and most expensive restaurants in Austin, Texas, and ordered a bottle of zinfandel. She would have also liked to order dinner, but Gina was only here as a place holder for Monica Teague, her insanely busy employer. Monica was a professional fund-raiser, something Gina had never heard of until she became her personal assistant. Gina's job was to be another set of arms, legs, eyes and ears for Monica. To think for Monica. To *be* Monica when Monica couldn't be Monica.

Like now. Monica was supposed to meet Ford O'Banion, her fiancé, here for dinner. She was running late, so she'd sent Gina to hold the table in case Ford was running late, too.

And he was, no surprise there.

The wine arrived and Gina had the waiter pour her a glass. She'd changed the dinner reservation four times already. The only reason she'd gotten a table tonight was that she'd stretched the truth and said that Monica and Ford wanted to sample the food because they were considering having their wedding reception at Lily's.

"So you want a chef's tasting menu." The hostess's voice had warmed and Gina had guessed that a tasting menu was expensive.

"That sounds wonderful," Gina had told her. She was in no position to refuse.

So when Monica started calling from her meeting late this afternoon, Gina informed her that somebody was going to have to keep this reservation, or Monica and Ford would never dine at Lily's again.

As Gina sipped her wine, her Monica cell vibrated. Gina carried two phones. One was exclusively for calls from Monica, or for when she asked Gina to make calls on her behalf and wanted her own name to appear on caller ID. The other, a handy iPhone, was Gina's. "Hi, Monica."

"Is Ford there yet?"

"No."

"Good. I don't know when I'll be able to get away. These people can*not* make up their minds. Keep him company for me until I can get there, okay?"

"Will do."

As Gina punched off one cell phone, the other buzzed. It was Ford, Monica's fiancé.

And Gina's crush.

"Hey, Gina, is she there?"

Even distorted by the speakerphone in his car, his voice made her smile. "Not yet."

"Whoo. Good. I just left Round Rock so, depending on traffic, I'm about forty-five minutes out."

"Wow." Gina had already stalled for a half hour and the waitstaff was hovering and sending anxious glances toward the kitchen.

"I know, I know. Do me a favor and order a calla lily for the table, would you, Gina?"

"Sure."

"Thanks, I owe you." His typical sign-off.

He owed her a lot, actually. And the closer the wedding drew, the more favors he casually asked of her. She knew he had no idea how many little, and not so little, tasks and errands she'd performed on his behalf, and she knew she'd keep doing them because then she had an excuse to interact with him.

Was that not pathetic?

Gina had fallen hard for the man who was going to become her boss's husband. And no wonder—she saw him more than Monica did.

Ford O'Banion was founder and CEO of O'Banion Green, an environmental-consulting company. Going green was hot right now, and Ford was as insanely busy as Monica.

The two of them had met last year at a green fund-raiser Monica had put together. Ford had been one of the sponsors.

For several weeks, they'd seen each other every day and had become disgustingly besotted. Gina missed those days. She'd actually had some free time—whole evenings when the Monica cell didn't buzz.

Gina took a swallow of wine. Ford's favorite.

The campaign had ended in a celebratory Festival of Green and that night, caught up in the high of a successful fund-raiser, Monica and Ford decided to get married.

Ever since, they'd been trying to mesh schedules—with Gina acting as chief mesher.

She liked them both. She did. Well, she liked Ford in a different, completely inappropriate way, but they both deserved happiness. They were good people doing good things.

Gina signaled one of the waitstaff and ordered the calla lily, a signature offering of the restaurant. It was also Monica's favorite flower.

The Monica cell buzzed. Gina sipped her wine before answering it. "Hi."

"Is he there?"

"He's on his way."

Monica exhaled. "Shoot."

Gina knew what that meant. "Suggest they take a dinner break." The strategy had worked with overly long meetings before.

"I did. They've ordered deli boxes."

"Leave and come back?"

"Maybe. Let me think."

Poor Monica. So many times she worked with volunteers and nonprofessionals who used the meetings as social gatherings. That was fine for them, but a time sink for Monica.

She was very, very good at what she did and Gina was proud to be a member of team Monica. Because of Monica's ideas and leadership, millions of dollars had been raised for dozens of worthy causes. Monica worked on a flat-fee structure and groups sometimes balked. This was for charity—she shouldn't charge for charity work, they thought. Monica would point out that it was the business of raising money, and the truth was that they would raise more with professional guidance than without it. Sometimes a group was ready to make a commitment and sometimes there were vocal holdouts, as there were tonight.

Then it became a gamble—invest more time by sticking around to answer questions or cut and run.

That would be one of the few issues Gina had with her boss. Monica didn't know when to walk away.

The calla lily arrived in a tall vase that soared above the table. The waiter addressed her. "The chef has asked me if he could begin serving while you wait for your other party. As you know, we allow two hours for a tasting menu and we're already somewhat behind schedule."

"I am so sorry. They were unavoidably detained."

"The chef is concerned that his food will not be presented to its best advantage."

Gina could imagine the behind-the-scenes drama going on in the kitchen. And darn it, she was hungry. "I understand. Please tell him to start."

Clearly relieved, the waiter hurried to the kitchen. Gina hated to think what was going to happen when the chef realized that half the food would end up in Styrofoam boxes in Monica's office fridge.

The first course arrived almost immediately—an amuse-bouche of a tiny deviled quail egg sitting in a spoon.

There were two of them.

Gina ate them both.

Next came a platter of various cold fish dishes, two of each, along with a menu card identifying each one. Obviously, the chef was trying to hurry things along as well as offer as wide a selection as he could.

Gina felt a few pangs of guilt, but the hunger pangs were stronger. She scanned the card, trying to identify the two eyes staring at her. "Smoked salmon with caviar on a sliver of brioche with crème fraîche." Okay, except that she couldn't imagine dozens of them appearing at a wedding dinner. Gina ate a zucchini blossom stuffed with crab and truffle butter. Okay, now that was better. She skipped the grilled octopus, and selected two of several fancy tunas with long names and something that looked and tasted like a potato chip, but was apparently something else.

Then she rearranged the plate so it wouldn't look so snacked upon. In doing so, she knocked over an artful tower of scallops, polenta rounds, heirloom tomatoes and some wilted green stuff propped up with a couple of chives. So she ate the evidence.

The food was *really* good. With her phone, Gina took a picture of the remaining samples on the platter, including the eyes. Monica hadn't used Lily's to cater any fund-raisers in the Austin area. Maybe she should consider them.

She was making notes on the menu card when something made her look up.

And there he was, Ford O'Banion, weaving through the tables, a smile on his face for *her.* Because she, Gina, was sitting here, eating his food and drinking his wine, and Monica was not.

She drank in the sight of his endearingly smile-creased face

and sympathized with the end-of-day tiredness she saw behind
the smile. He was the type of guy who should be on the floor
of his family room playing with a couple of kids and a puppy.
Who would share a look with her before whisking them off for
their bath—the puppy, too. She'd prepare their dinner accompanied by happy shrieks and laughter. Then they'd both tuck
their babies in bed, smiling at the angelic little darlings. Then
he would take her in his arms, murmur, "At last," and they'd
never get around to eating dinner.

Yes, Gina needed serious therapy.

"Hi." Ford unbuttoned his jacket before he sat, and cast a
quick look around. "Is Monica in the ladies' room or…?"

"She's…not here. Yet." *But I am! I am!*

He picked up the bottle of wine, looked at the label, smiled
to himself and refilled Gina's glass.

That was very generous of him, Gina thought, since she'd
already drunk a glass—maybe a glass and a half.

"Do we have an ETA?" he asked as he waved away the assistant waiter and poured his own glass.

"We do not. The clients she's meeting with have been slow
to come to a decision."

He gave a short nod and surveyed the table. "What do we
have here?"

Gina had decimated the platter. "I ordered a tasting menu
and the chef needed to begin service." She showed him the
menu card with her notes. "Oh, and he might have the idea that
you're considering having your reception here."

Ford ate one of the salmon eyes. "Are we?"

"No," Gina whispered. "We are placating a restaurant that
we've canceled on three times."

"Gotcha." He studied the card. "Octopus. Nothing says I
love you like grilled octopus."

Gina chortled. "Personally, I thought the eyes were a little
Halloweeny."

"Yeah. I don't like my food looking at me." Ford ate the other one.

Gina allowed herself a little, meltingly tender, inward sigh. She needed to snap out of it, she truly did. But not yet. After the wedding was soon enough.

The Monica cell buzzed with an incoming text. Gina had been holding it in her lap and glanced down to read the message.

Still discussing. Ford there?

Yes, Gina texted back.

Thot he'd cancel. Tell him I'll make it up to him.

Gina stared at her screen. Monica had stored that last line in her macros, she'd had to use it so often.

She looked up to find Ford watching her. "She's not coming, is she?"

"The meeting is still going on. It started at four o'clock and we knew it was going to go long when they ordered in dinner, but Monica felt that—"

"Don't explain."

"She said to tell you that she'll make it up to you."

"It's not a big deal."

Gina thought it should be, although to be fair, Ford had canceled a number of times himself. Gina shouldn't be so judgmental. It was the nature of their careers that much of his and Monica's face-to-face meeting time with clients took place after regular work hours and on weekends.

Reaching for her purse, she dropped the cell phone in its pocket and put her napkin by her plate.

"Hey, don't go. Unless Monica…?"

"No. I'm done for the day." Or what was left of it.

"Gina! Stay and finish your dinner." He waved at the nearly empty platter.

He didn't need to ask her twice. Gina put her purse down and reached for her napkin.

"I'd hoped that Monica and I could discuss our housing situation." Ford brought out a map and several brochures as the waitstaff cleared away the platter and replaced it with the next course, a lamb lollipop on a bed of something green and curly.

Monica and Ford could not agree on where they were going to live. Monica's town house was near her office, which was in the arty social area of Austin. Ford's home was a small, specially constructed "green" house on the far outskirts of Austin in a mostly undeveloped area.

Austin's tangle of traffic and unfinished highway construction was notorious. Whoever moved would have a tedious commute.

Both parties had vented to Gina. Monica felt she had the ideal location for her business, and moving so far out of town would hinder her legendary networking.

Ford's house was an example of his passion and his business. He couldn't live in a house that hadn't been built to make the smallest carbon footprint possible. He'd be a hypocrite.

This was a toughie. To Gina, the obvious solution was to build green in Monica's area. But there weren't any available housing lots, and anyway, there wasn't enough time before the wedding.

Ford spread the brochures out so they faced Gina. "There's a new subdivision going up not far from here and I've been consulting with them. Mark, the owner, flat-out asked me what kind of home he'd have to build before I would buy it. And so, we went back and forth, and—" Ford unfolded the paper stapled to one of the brochures "—came up with this."

Gina looked at the simple floor-plan drawing of a three-bedroom house. It looked like any other house plan she had seen, but she was no expert.

Ford grinned. "Looks like nothing special, right?"

"Well, yeah."

He pointed to a curving line. "That's the side of the hill. The back part of the house will be built into the limestone and stay at the same temperature year-round without using electricity or gas."

He expounded more on all the sustainable features the new house would have, his enthusiasm making him even more attractive. No wonder Monica had fallen for him.

No wonder Gina had.

"So won't Monica love this?" He was beaming.

No. Monica would not. Gina would have given anything to tell him what he wanted to hear. "Monica will love the idea, but she's not going to want to live in a cave."

2

"THIS BACK SECTION is not going to be like living in a cave!" Ford laughed as though amazed anyone would think so. "There will be skylights. The front third of the house is all outside like any other house. I promise, you won't even know you're in the side of a hill."

Monica would never go for it. Never, never, never.

Even Gina, with her images of puppies, wet, wiggly children and a Ford with eyes only for her, would have to be talked into it.

"There have been such phenomenal developments in sustainable construction materials," Ford told her. "And this way, Monica could decorate with environmentally friendly fabrics and low-VOC paints. I know how much being a good steward of our planet means to her." He gazed into the middle distance. "When I saw her wearing that dress made of Eco Intelligent polyester at the Festival of Green, that was just it for me. I knew she was the one."

Because of a dress? *That* dress? He wanted to marry Monica because she wore a dress *one* time? The polyester was more intelligent than he was.

Crush or not, his cluelessness made Gina want to stab him with her fork. She wanted to stab Monica, as well, but Ford was here and Monica wasn't.

Monica didn't care about the environment. Okay, that wasn't true. Of course she *cared,* but she wasn't an environmental activist. Gina had been the one who'd shopped all over for a "green" dress. She and Monica wore the same size—a factor in Gina's hiring, she knew—and Gina had been the one forced to try on poorly made dresses in stiff, wrinkled, organic cotton and hemp in drab colors. Or thin, limp bamboo with puckered seams. Did responsible have to mean ugly? And just finding a dress that wasn't too casual or emblazoned with a tree-hugging slogan had been nearly impossible. But she'd finally found one in a golden-brown fabric with a little sheen to it and had the tailor cut off the sleeves. Monica had pronounced it barely acceptable and vowed never to wear it again. It was currently hanging in Gina's closet.

Ford could be excused for overestimating Monica's commitment to the green movement. The thing was, Monica immersed herself in whatever cause had hired her as a fund-raiser. When the campaign was over, she moved on. It was no reflection on the worthiness of a goal or charity. Monica was a professional and there were many worthy goals and charities.

Ford should have picked up on that by now.

It was not Gina's place to enlighten him. She wasn't sure it was her place to enlighten *Monica.* Maybe she'd give her a heads-up, but that was it.

If ever two people needed to have a serious meeting of the minds, it was these two.

While Gina had been thinking, and Ford had continued talking about the future with Monica as he saw it, the chef had sent out yet more courses. Grilled fallow deer medallions and blueberry-pepper-encrusted wild boar. Oh, why not?

Ford picked up the brochures (printed on recycled paper with soy ink) and put them back in his inside jacket pocket. "I'd give these to you to show her, but I'd like to see her face, you know?"

Gina wanted to see her face, too. "Let's sync schedules." She got out her iPhone and accessed the calendar.

Ford withdrew his BlackBerry. "Try to find a free afternoon. I'll take her to lunch and afterward, we can look at the property."

There was no such thing as a free afternoon in Monica's schedule. There were only things that could be moved and things that could not be moved. "How about meeting late in the afternoon on Thursday? You could drive out, see the property and then have dinner."

Ford shook his head. "I'll be in Dallas."

They continued going back and forth through a course of some kind of duck that Gina thought was a bit on the pink side. She stopped and photographed it, as she had been doing with all the others.

"Was lunch on the eighteenth the last time you two saw each other?" she asked.

"Actually, we missed each other that day," he confessed. "I ran late and Monica had to leave early."

Gina looked up at him. "When was the last time you and Monica saw each other? Actually saw each other. Face-to-face."

"I don't know…three weeks? Maybe a month. It's been crazy."

No, you two are crazy. "Then we'd better make something happen."

"Saturday. Pick a Saturday," Ford told her. "In fact, pick a whole weekend. We'll make it a wedding-marathon weekend and take care of all the details we've been putting off."

Gina hesitated. It would take some shuffling. "She has her fitting for her wedding gown Saturday after next and I absolutely can't reschedule that. Not again."

"Okay—then I'll meet her afterward."

Slowly, Gina nodded and blocked off the time on Monica's calendar.

And then she and Ford thoroughly enjoyed a mini crème brûlée and a torchon of chocolate ganache with sea salt and olive oil drizzled on top.

ON THE SATURDAY after next, from the flybridge of a sinfully wasteful but heavenly motor yacht, Ford watched the coastline of Lake Travis ease by. This morning, he'd received a call from Monica canceling their plans.

"Gina told me you couldn't move your fitting," he'd said.

"Gina will find a way. It's still three months until the wedding—how much time does it take to sew a hem and replace a few beads? The salon just wants to make a big deal out of it to justify the price of the dress. Anyway, I've got to go. Gina will call you to reschedule." And she'd hung up.

That last bit rankled. "Gina will call you to reschedule," she'd said as though he were an irritating client and not the man she'd agreed to marry.

Sure, Ford had canceled before. But this was different. They were supposed to be finding a place to live and they were running out of time. Mark Crawley had offered to meet them here at the site and explain his vision of Green River Homes. He'd gone to the trouble of making mock-ups.

They could have first pick of the lots. First. Pick.

Ford felt worse when he saw that Mark had brought his motor yacht so he could take Monica around the area in the lake.

"There it is." Mark pointed to a sliver of undeveloped land fronting the lake. "I bought that lot from the owners of the house on the left. Now I can build a community boat dock and ensure the residents have convenient access to the lake. Otherwise, they'll have to pay for privileges at the marina a couple of miles away."

Ford patted the cushy chair—vinyl just oozing chemicals into the atmosphere—and gestured to his surroundings. "They can't park something like this at a community dock."

Mark smiled. "No. This baby lives in her covered slip at the marina."

Ford looked directly behind the lot Mark had bought and up into the hills where he hoped to build the Green Lake subdivision.

"I'm a little uncomfortable with the concept of sustainable living and a motor yacht." He was appalled that Mark owned such a thing, to tell the truth.

"I've been waiting for you to bring that up. You're absolutely right. So." Mark grinned at him. "How about we start a company making green pleasure craft? You design and I'll implement. Realistically, people aren't going to deprive themselves of everything they enjoy. But we can offer them a more eco-friendly way to have fun."

Ford felt a little pop of interest, the same little pop he always felt at a good idea. "Mark, I'm a landlubber from west Texas. I don't know anything about boats."

"You can learn." Mark rounded one of the hundreds of bends in the snakelike lake. "And the field's wide open."

"It sounds intriguing." That was Ford's standard stalling response.

Mark recognized it for what it was. "Tell you what. Let me know when you can corral that fiancée of yours and I'll lend you the *Sarah June*. Best way to learn what's important on a boat and what you can't mess with is to spend a couple of days on the water." He slid a sideways glance at Ford. "You two can have a romantic getaway. Even better, I'll show you the places on the lake where there's no cell-phone reception."

The man did know how to negotiate. "You know what, Mark? You've just made me an offer I can't refuse."

TWO WEEKS LATER, Gina sat in the parking lot of Elizabeth Gray Bridal Salon in Rocky Falls. Alone. Monica had flown to Nashville early that morning to present a fund-raising proposal to an arm of the music industry. She wasn't even in the same time zone anymore.

Gina was checking for an e-mail from Ford. After Monica had canceled her fitting and her outing with him two weeks ago, there had been a drop in the number of e-mails and texts. Those that were sent had a distinctly chilly tone.

E-mailing Ford was Gina's guilty pleasure. It had started months ago with Monica saying, "E-mail Ford that I'll be late—make it nice. You know." So Gina embellished the unpleasant info, and when Ford responded, she'd responded, and they were off. Gina knew that he thought he was e-mailing and texting Monica. And, in her mind, she was only saying what Monica would say if Monica had time. But Monica had Gina and that was Gina's job and…and it was amazing how easy it was for Gina to justify her guilty pleasure.

The entire record of their correspondence was there for Monica to see, but Gina knew she didn't keep up with it, so if Ford said anything Monica really needed to know—such as having an aunt in the hospital, or inviting her to dinner with friends—Gina informed her at their daily briefing.

The shared jokes, the extra tidbits of interaction, Gina just enjoyed. After Monica and Ford were married, she would miss this, because she most definitely could not continue. No way did she want to get one of those "You were incredible last night" e-mails. Blech.

Ford had been angry when Monica canceled two weeks ago, and when Gina had called to reschedule, he'd vented. Gina had alerted Monica, but she'd just closed her eyes in weariness.

"I can't deal with that now. Gina? Can you…?"

And Gina knew she was supposed to smooth things over on Monica's behalf. "I'll do my best."

But things weren't smooth at all.

Gina stared at the entrance to the salon. Things weren't smooth on the wedding front, either.

Monica wouldn't accept that she couldn't reschedule her fitting again. After all, hadn't she canceled the uncancelable two weeks ago? And hadn't Gina come through with yet another appointment?

"They've got two months," Monica had said. "Offer to pay them a rush fee."

"We're already paying them a rush fee because we broke your last appointment," Gina reminded her. "They absolutely refuse to book you another fitting. There's a huge wedding party scheduled and the seamstresses will be working on those dresses. You'll have to find your own tailor if you don't keep Saturday's appointment."

Monica exhaled. "Then you'll have to do it."

"What?"

"Keep the appointment. We're the same size. I have to try the dress on after the alterations have been done anyway, and they can tweak the fit then. I don't know why I didn't think of that before!"

"That's—"

"Gina, I'm counting on you." Monica had gripped her shoulder. "Make this happen."

So here she was, making this happen. Gina got out of the car and entered the salon. At least she didn't have to endure another horrible conversation with Ford. When she'd called to tell him about today's fitting and see if he wanted to try the same schedule as before, he'd declined, saying they'd just play it by ear.

He'd turned down a chance to see Monica. Did Monica even notice that two weeks had gone by without her breaking a date with Ford because there had been no dates to break?

Gina had noticed. She missed talking to him and couldn't shake the feeling that he was angry with *her* because she'd told him Monica had an unbreakable appointment. Now that Monica had bailed on this one, too, Gina was very glad Ford had declined.

"I'm here for Monica Teague's appointment," she said to the receptionist.

Gina had hoped she could just slip in and get fitted, but Lia, the assistant manager, busted her.

After an unpleasant conversation, Lia handed her an alterations release form that basically said that the customer had asked for work to be done against the advice of the salon and therefore, the salon wasn't responsible, etc., etc. "After you sign, I'll make you a copy."

Signing the release was the only way Lia would agree to use Gina as a fit model. Gina didn't blame her.

Lia led Gina to a large room in the back where she had to put on uncomfortable underwear of the type women had liberated themselves from wearing. As if that weren't enough, Monica's dress required hoops.

After she was trussed like an extra in a *Gone with the Wind* remake, an older woman carried the dress in. "Monica Teague?" Rather than explain, which would require breathing, Gina nodded. "You're one busy lady."

"Tell me about it," Gina mumbled, and stepped into the dress.

Once the thousand or so tiny covered buttons were in their loops, she stood on the pedestal and faced the pathetic image of herself wearing the wedding dress of the woman who was going to marry the man Gina loved.

THE MAN GINA LOVED was in the corresponding fitting room on the other side of the wall.

"Monica Teague?" he heard. "You're one busy lady."

So Monica had really, actually kept today's appointment. Ford exhaled and smiled. He couldn't make out the mumbled response, but an image of Gina flashed in his mind, not surprising since in past weeks, he'd seen Gina more than Monica.

But that was going to change. He and Monica needed to reconnect. Or disconnect. Yes, he loved her e-mails and texts, but when he spoke to her on the phone, she was always abrupt or in the middle of something or couldn't talk. He knew she composed the e-mails and texts when she had a chunk of time, probably sitting in meetings. That was the Monica he loved and the Monica he wanted to marry. So, since she needed time to be that Monica, he was giving her that time. And he wasn't giving her a chance to refuse.

"Step into the dress and I'll fasten you."

There were rustling sounds. "There are a lot of buttons. But worth it. Ooooh, you look so beautiful!"

Ford motioned to the two teenagers sitting in the dressing room with him. "Okay, she's in there," he whispered. "I'm leaving to get things set up. You two wait here until she's done and then hurry over to the salon before she gets away."

Ford's coconspirators were Mark's seventeen-year-old son and his friend Brian. They nodded.

"You can't let her get away—if she gets in her car, it's all over," Ford emphasized.

"Got it," one said.

Ford held a finger to his lips. When he'd been fitted with his tux, he remembered hearing the conversations from the women's dressing room in the bridal salon and figured he'd put the lack of soundproofing to good use. He'd explained his plan to a sympathetic salesclerk named J.C., who checked to see if Monica was scheduled for the fitting room on the other side, and then let the three of them camp out in here.

He went over the sequence of events with the boys once more. "Remember, hand her the calla lily from me, issue the invitation and then escort her to the car. Do not take no for an answer. Do not let her use her cell phone. She will argue, she will complain, she might be mad. No…she *will* be mad. Count on that. She will threaten. Do not speak to her. Do not stop driving until you reach the marina. Got that?"

"Yeah," they whispered, and grinned at each other. "This is so cool!" Mark's son said aloud.

"Okay." Ford stood. "Call me if the plan goes south."

3

"THIS IS SO COOL!" Gina heard a young male voice say.

She smiled at the woman pinning the seams. "They must be renting tuxes for their prom. I wonder what they think is cool?"

"The boys like the jackets with the tails sometimes." She finished the pinning and eyed the bodice. "How does it feel under the arms?" Hitching at the strapless top, she frowned. "It looks like it cuts into the skin a little bit."

So Gina had been hitting the bagels a little too hard. Monica hadn't. "It's fine."

"You sure?"

"Yes," Gina said firmly.

"Okay, let's do the hem. Did you bring your wedding shoes?"

Gina looked at the woman blankly. No, she had not brought Monica's wedding shoes. Monica didn't have wedding shoes, Gina suspected. Monica certainly didn't have the right wedding underwear. "No," she said, but the tailor was already tsking.

"Do you know what height heel you plan to wear?"

"Um…a comfortable height?"

The woman glanced at the leather flip-flops Gina had worn with her capris. "I have some one-inch boards that you can stand on. We'll stack as many as you think we need and pin the hem that way."

"Sounds like a plan!" Gina gave her an overly enthusiastic smile and dug out her phone as soon as the woman left the room.

The call went immediately to Monica's voice mail, which

meant she hadn't turned it back on. Gina left a message telling her if she didn't hear back, she was going for two-inch heels.

She should not be here making these decisions for Monica. This was her *wedding* dress. Didn't she care?

If Gina were marrying Ford, she'd want everything to be perfect. She certainly wouldn't send her assistant to stand in for her as though it was just another chore.

But Gina wasn't marrying Ford. She inhaled as deeply as she could. Then she blew out her breath. Time to detach. She'd been miserable not talking to him the past two weeks and she had to get over it. What she felt was infatuation, not love. It couldn't be love unless the other person loved you back.

And the other person would never love you back if all you ever did was make the wrong woman look like the right woman.

Gina stared at herself. If Monica wanted to marry Ford, then she needed to act like it. And if Ford wanted to marry Monica, then he needed to deal directly with Monica, not with Gina pretending to be Monica.

She was done.

Gina couldn't stand being in this poufy meringue of a dress another second. She just couldn't. She jumped off the pedestal, slipped on the flip-flops the tailor had dismissed and billowed after the woman. If Monica needed her dress hemmed, then she was going to have to find a tailor to do it. Or Gina would. But Gina would rather phone a hundred tailors than wear this dress a second longer.

Mirrors mocked her as she stormed through the dressing area and emerged into the main salon. Where was the woman she'd been working with? Or somebody who could help her get out of this stupid dress. She looked around uncertainly.

A breathless young man entered the salon. "Monica Teague?"

Startled, Gina looked his way and saw that he carried a single calla lily. It could only have come from Ford.

She felt tears. Stupid tears. Pointless tears.

"Monica Teague?" He looked around the salon, saw her staring at him and took a tentative step toward her. "Monica Teague?"

Her job was to be Monica when Monica couldn't be Monica. Gina walked toward him. "Is that from Ford?"

"Yes, ma'am." He handed the calla lily to her. "He invites you to join him for dinner. I'm here to escort you."

Gina nearly crushed the stem of the flower. "I'm sorry, but I can't."

The boy took her arm and urged her toward the door. "No, really," Gina insisted. "Please tell Ford that Monica has other plans this evening."

"He said that you would refuse."

That was just sad. The boy still held her arm and they'd reached the door. "You don't understand. I'm not going with you."

"Mr. O'Banion said that we weren't to take no for an answer." And he pulled her through the salon door.

"Hey! Wait! Are you nuts? I'm still wearing the wedding dress!"

"Sorry, but we have our orders."

Orders?

He pulled her toward a Lincoln Continental parked in front of the shop. Another boy sat in the driver's seat.

"Stop it!" Gina demanded. "You're going to damage the dress."

"Then stop struggling and get into the car, ma'am."

"No!"

The driver got out and came to join the other boy. Gina became truly alarmed. She braced her feet and splayed her arms across the car as both boys pushed.

In the end, the stupid corset, the hoops and about a hundred yards of tulle did her in. She sprawled face-first into the backseat, the hoops of the dress scraping against the ceiling. She tried screaming for help, but had left it too late and couldn't get a good breath, anyway.

They'd lulled her with the calla lily. Gina righted herself and batted the dress into submission as the car took off. The skirt rose until she could barely see over the top. She squashed it and tried to contain it between her knees as it mounded on either side of her.

Her heart pounded hard against the boning of the corset.

"Am I being kidnapped?" Actually, Gina supposed it was Monica who was being kidnapped.

"No. You're being escorted."

"I don't want to be escorted."

"Mr. O'Banion said you wouldn't cooperate and we weren't to listen to you."

"Well, listen to this—I'm not Monica Teague. You've kidnapped the wrong bride, Sherlock."

They laughed. "That's pretty good."

"And it's pretty true. Hand over your cell phone and I'll call Ford and straighten this out."

They both shook their heads. "He said not to let you use *your* phone."

"I don't have my phone. I want to use *your* phone."

"No, he—"

"Call him. *Call* him! Call him right this minute!" Sometimes people responded to the voice of authority.

"Mr. O'Banion said you'd be mad."

And sometimes not. "Mr. O'Banion has no idea." Gina sank back into the leather seat and tried to catch her breath. Okay, she probably wasn't being kidnapped. This was Ford's way of not giving Monica a chance to cancel. She had to admire his take-charge plan, but he needed to work on the execution.

"Where are we going?" she asked, trying another tack.

"Uh…" They glanced at each other.

"I think it's supposed to be a surprise," one said.

"But you'll love it," added the driver.

"How far away is the surprise?"

"Probably about an hour and twenty minutes."

Over an hour away from her clothes, her purse and her phone? And she was wearing a pinned-up wedding gown. Not even her own. "Guys—get real. I'm in a wedding gown! I'm hardly dressed for dinner in a restaurant."

"We're not taking you to a restaurant—" The driver poked the boy who'd given her the flower.

"You'll like where you're going," he said. "It's awesome. I've, uh, spent some time there."

"Could we at least go back so I can get my purse? If I promise not to run away?"

"No," they chorused. "And we're not supposed to be talking to you, anyway."

"This is ridiculous! Will you just call Ford? You don't even have to let me talk to him. I'll yell from the backseat."

Silence.

"What's he paying you?" she asked.

"He's not *paying* us," one said. "He's helping with our Science Fair booth."

"Quit talking to her!" said the other.

Gina gave up. "Okay. You win. But when Ford sees me and gets mad, remember that I told you that I'm not Monica Teague."

What a waste of a perfectly good Saturday.

Gina half expected the salon to call the police. How could a woman in full bridal regalia be taken out the front door and, in full view of the main salon, be forced into an admittedly plush Lincoln without anyone noticing?

And yet, over an hour of uneventful travel later, they were driving toward the Lakeway Marina.

Ford must have wanted to take Monica sailing. Even if she were Monica, her wedding dress would have put a crimp in that plan. Ford was lucky she wasn't Monica. Monica would never forgive him.

The boys parked in front of a covered slip with a fancy boat named the *Sarah June* parked—moored?—in it.

The driver made a call. "Package delivery."

Gina rolled her eyes.

They got out of the car and opened both sides of the back. "Uh." Then both doors slammed shut again.

Gina snickered.

One door opened. "If you'll step this way, ma'am."

And she was going to get out of the car how? As soon as she relaxed her knees, the dress popped up. Gina tried to maneuver her way across the seat and got stabbed by a pin for her effort. "I could use some help."

They looked at each other.

"It's not a trick! I am resigned to my fate, if you will. So help me out of the car and let's get this over with."

The dress was so big, Gina couldn't see her feet and had to step blindly onto the concrete walkway. There was a sad little ripping sound as some beading caught in the door, but, levering herself with the boys' help, she made it out okay. She maybe only flashed them twice.

They each held on to one of her arms. "I'm not going to run." She yanked her arms away. "See?" She walked toward the little gangway, dress billowing in the wind. Actually, it didn't need wind to billow. "This is me not running."

When she reached the part where she was going to have to step onto some slick-looking fiberglass, she said, "I can't see my feet. If I slip and fall in, do not hesitate. Jump in after me. I can't swim in this."

"Wait just a sec." The boy who'd driven clambered on board and held out his hands.

Gina took one and propped herself on the other boy's shoulder. "This is what they call a leap of faith." She stepped as far as she could, having no idea where her foot would land.

The boning dug into her and the boy had to really pull, but Gina got aboard without falling in and without losing her flip-flops.

She was perched on the aft sundeck and she assumed Ford was in the pilothouse in the front.

The boy gestured. "See the door down those steps?"

"That tiny little thing?"

"Uh, yeah. It goes to the living area belowdecks. You should probably wait in there."

How was she supposed to get herself and this monstrosity of a dress through the door?

Gina squashed her dress and gingerly made her way down the steps, ignoring little clicking noises that sounded like beads falling on fiberglass. She didn't want to know. Pulling open the door, she found more steps.

Gina was trying to figure out whether to try climbing down frontward or backward when the yacht began moving. She heard shouting and felt a bump that sent her tumbling down a step. She grabbed at the railing and stopped herself from falling, but not from stepping on the dress and tearing it at the waist. Beads scattered.

Monica was going to flip out.

Gina hitched up as much fabric as she could gather and descended sideways into a surprisingly spacious area. A vase of calla lilies greeted her and Gina sighed. Calla lilies were regally beautiful and elegant, but she was a yellow-rose gal herself. However, Ford had bought those for Monica, not for her.

Gina walked into a living area with a larger TV than she owned, and a kitchen with real granite countertops. Two shiny wooden tables were parked in front of a banquette and beyond that, she guessed she'd find the sleeping quarters.

The first door she opened was the master suite and she looked no further. It had a queen-size bed with her name on it, the only thing large enough to support both her and the dress. As for the bathroom—forget it. Just forget it.

In fact, she was ready to forget all of this. Ford's lovely romantic getaway was ruined. The dress was ruined. To be honest, the engagement was ruined. Gina suspected her job would be collateral damage.

She sat on the bed and fell backward so the corset would stop digging into her stomach. The dress popped up like her own personal igloo. Anyone could see her underwear.

She did not care.

WHEN MONICA DIDN'T COME to find him in the pilothouse, Ford knew she was angry.

When half an hour floated by, he knew she was furious. Ford didn't feel experienced enough to abandon the controls without anchoring the boat, so he kept going. He was headed directly toward one of the dead-cell zones Mark had told him about. It was still about a half hour away, especially at the slow speed at which Ford felt most comfortable, but he didn't want to leave Monica alone any longer. He'd probably be taking her back, anyway. He'd better stop right now.

As he dropped anchor, he imagined Gina's reaction. He could hear her saying, "Way to go!" In fact, why didn't he just call her right now and hear her say, "Way to go!" and then tell him how he should approach Monica?

Gina didn't pick up.

Disappointed, Ford went below to face Monica. When he didn't find her in the salon, he realized she might be in the bed, waiting for him.

Of course she was! He was an idiot. Ford jogged to the master suite, only to be puzzled by what looked like a white pup tent with a pair of bare legs hanging over the side of the bed.

"Monica?"

Two arms smashed down the white tent and a torso rose stiffly to an upright position.

"Gina!"

"The man who can't hire competent thugs, I presume?"

Ford stared at her, vaguely registering that she was angry. He was stunned and not because she was here and Monica wasn't, but because he was glad she was here and Monica wasn't.

He shouldn't feel that way, but there was no doubt that he did.

"Gina." Instantly, he was aware of a shuffling in his memory as his synapses rearranged the past few weeks with a different focus. Talking with Gina, conspiring with Gina, eating dinner with Gina, laughing with Gina.

He gazed at her, taking in her bare shoulders and creamy skin, the plump curves above the neckline and the fascinating way they moved, caused by her quick, angry breathing. With her bare feet, she looked like a naughty princess in the billowy white dress.

The billowy white *wedding* dress.

This was not going to end well.

4

"STOP STARING and get me out of this dress!" Gina hopped off the bed and turned around. "You aren't even supposed to *see* it before the wedding!"

Ford looked at a long row of buttons and loops. "I…"

Gina pushed her hair out of the way, revealing her neck. "Just start at the top and keep going. I can hardly breathe and I can't get out of this thing by myself!"

Ford started at the top, his fingers brushing her bare skin. Gina's bare skin. He swallowed against a really, really unwanted urge to turn her around and kiss her.

The loops were tight and the buttons didn't want to slip through easily. This was going to take a long time and unless he distracted himself, he didn't have a long time before he did something stupid. "Where's Monica?"

"Nashville."

Actually, he found he didn't care where Monica was. He barely remembered what she looked like.

The first button was free. The next was easier. By the third, he was getting the hang of it, but not getting the hang of seeing more of Gina's back. To distract himself, he said, "This boat belongs to Mark, the guy who's building Green River Homes. His son was one of the boys who—"

"Kidnapped me out of a bridal salon?"

"That wasn't kidnapping, that was 'whisking,' as in 'whisking away for a romantic weekend.'"

"Oh, well, that makes it all better, then."

Ford had never heard Gina angry and sarcastic before. "Okay, look, I know you're angry. I'm sorry. But what are you doing in Monica's wedding dress?"

"Don't you try to make this my fault!"

What? "I only asked! It's a reasonable question."

"Well, obviously, I'm getting it fitted because we wear the same size and Monica couldn't break another appointment. Of course, thanks to you, the dress is going to take a lot of work before anybody gets married in it. It's ripped, beads are missing, the bottom is dirty and there's a lovely black oil streak from the car door."

Somewhere in his mind, a voice whispered that it would be an excuse to postpone the wedding. "The boys shouldn't have taken you while you were wearing the dress. Next time, they'll know better."

"*Next* time?" Gina turned her head and glared at him.

He hadn't seen her glare before, either. "I messed up," he told her. "I'm sorry."

"You don't sound sorry." She turned back around.

Because he wasn't. He was here, undressing her, having wildly inappropriate thoughts and urges. Ford continued working the buttons and encountered a stiff lace shell. "What is this thing?"

"A corset. As soon as you can, undo the hooks and the laces. It's killing me."

Ford worked faster until he got to the corset. The knots were tight and the lacing was wet because Gina had sweated. Far from being repelled, he wanted to bury his nose in her back.

Finally, he got the knots and laces loose and tugged at the hooks until the thing fell open, revealing Gina's naked back.

Unwanted desire coursed through him. Equally unwanted was the realization that another woman's naked back wouldn't do the same. Ford tried to imagine Monica's naked back. The surprise wasn't that he had trouble; it was that he didn't want to. He wanted the naked back in front of him to belong to Gina and Gina only.

Holding up the front of the corset, Gina gasped a lungful of air. "I am not wearing anything like this on my wedding day. I don't care how small it makes my waist looks."

Her waist was just fine. As she stood there breathing, Ford gazed at her smooth back, all the way down to her panties, which he saw through a circular cage. There were more buttons to unbutton, but Ford didn't trust himself to touch her.

"I think I can get out of this thing now. Can you lift it over my head?"

"Sure." Remarkably, his voice sounded normal. Ford pulled the heavy dress upward and dragged it sideways until Gina's head appeared.

"Thank you." She stood there in a see-through cage, clutching the open corset to her chest. "Can you untie the hoops now?"

He did so and she stepped out of them. They stayed standing. Ford nearly didn't. She was off-the-charts sexy, like an old-fashioned pinup girl.

"You're staring at me," she said.

"Yes. You're beautiful."

"I'm not Monica."

"I know."

She stepped closer to him and he felt certain vital functions nearing a meltdown. He wanted to reach for her. He was dizzy with wanting to touch her and hold her and drag the corset out of her hands.

Her eyes narrowed. "You do not get to look at me that way while you are engaged to be married to another woman."

She was right. He knew she was right. "You're beautiful whether or not I'm engaged."

Her expression didn't change. "It's time to call Monica. I'll get dressed and join you in the other room." She looked around. "I assume you packed a bag for her. Where is it?"

Clothes. Ford winced. Clothes weren't going to be important in his plans for the weekend.

"You didn't bring any clothes for her?" Gina asked incredulously.

"I bought a swimsuit. It's hanging in the bathroom," he told her.

Gina whipped around and stepped into the bathroom. Moments later, she stood in the doorway and dangled the suit from her finger. "So my choices are a wedding dress or a bikini?"

"Or nothing." He shouldn't have said that.

Gina pointed to the door.

"I'll go call Monica," Ford said hastily.

FORD WAS ON ONE of the sofas talking quietly to Monica when Gina entered the salon. She'd found a short cotton robe and had put it on over the navy and white bikini.

He was relieved, because for a few moments back there, he was having a damn-the-torpedoes-full-steam-ahead moment.

"Ford, what if I'd had people waiting on me and I just didn't show up? Did you think of that?" Monica said.

"You mean the way you don't show up for our meetings?"

"That's different."

"Not really."

"I have never stood you up!" she insisted. "I either leave you a message—"

"Or send Gina to placate me."

There was a significant silence. "Is she there?"

"Yes, she's here." Ford handed Gina the cell phone.

She refused. "Put it on speaker. I want to talk to both of you."

Ford did so and propped the phone in the cup holder on the little table.

"Monica?"

"Gina, are you okay?"

"Of course. But you two aren't," she declared. "You don't even know each other."

Ford was beginning to wonder if he knew himself.

"Gina, that's not—" Monica started.

"My business?" She started pacing, gesturing with her arms. "You both made it my business by using me as a go-between. I scheduled your dates. I canceled your dates. And I apologized to you on each other's behalf. You both used me as your confidant. I sent little mushy texts. One weird day, I sent and answered my own e-mails."

Ford stared at her. "You read my e-mails to Monica?"

"When she asked me to respond."

Monica's voice sounded over the phone. "Ford, Gina answers my routine e-mail."

Routine. She considered his e-mails routine? He glanced at Gina, but she kept her gaze fixed on the floor.

"You mean that sometimes when I thought I was texting Monica, I was texting you?" he asked her.

She looked up at him. "Don't sound so surprised. 'Gina, tell her I'm sorry and make it nice. You know what I mean.'"

Those were his words. He remembered tossing them off. They sounded so cold and uncaring now.

"Ford!" That was Monica. Like she was in any position to object.

He felt…many things. Appalled that he'd so casually involved Gina. Ashamed. And sad, because he'd shared his dreams and thoughts and…his personal stuff with her when he thought he'd been sharing with Monica.

But it got worse.

"You know that great bamboo desk set with the pens with environmentally friendly ink and the special pencils, Ford?" Gina asked. "I bought that for you. Monica, the black pearl earrings? I bought those. And I bought your birthday presents to each other, too."

"Gina!"

"All right. We get the idea," Ford said. He needed time to process everything.

"I'm not finished." Gina challenged him to interrupt her.

He didn't.

"You think you two know each other? Then tell me where you're going to live."

"That's part of what this weekend was about," Ford said. "I wanted Monica to choose a lot with me."

"What lot?" Monica asked.

"If you were ever around, you'd know," he snapped.

"Right," Gina said. "Talk about that in a minute. I've got one more thing to say and then I'll leave you both alone. Monica, going green isn't a fad Ford will outgrow. Ford, this isn't just a busy time Monica's going through. This is the way it always is. Her schedule and commitments aren't going to ease off. She'll never be a cozy homebody."

He'd already known that, hadn't he? From Monica's silence, he guessed she'd known it, too.

"Monica, from now on, your love life is no longer part of my duties. You'll have to handle it yourself." Gina walked toward the stairs. "I'm going topside to get some sun."

"Wait." There was something Ford had to know.

She looked back at him warily. This must have been hell for her.

"I'll call you back," he said to Monica and tossed the phone aside. "The conversations about movies—you or Monica?"

"Me."

"High school."

"Me."

"The size of our wedding?" He walked toward her.

"Me—but Monica told me what to say."

"About becoming vegan?"

"Me."

"The, uh, meat recipes?"

Gina smiled for the first time. "Oh, definitely me."

Ford reached the bottom of the stairs where she stood. "The green legislation?"

"Uh…" She shook her head. "That must have been Monica."

There had been no green-legislation conversation. Gina was telling the truth, not that he doubted her. It was just that Ford loved the woman with whom he'd exchanged thoughts and feelings. He thought it had been Monica, but it had been Gina.

So, how did Gina feel? She knew him so well and it seemed he knew her, but he hadn't known it was her, and this was all doing a number on his head.

They looked at each other as Ford tried to sort out his feelings. They hadn't gone away. They were just redirected. But it was a lot more complicated than switching numbers in his speed dial.

And he still didn't know if Gina felt anything for him at all, other than disgust and pity. Just because he was in love didn't mean she was. How could she be? How could he explain his monumental mistake? "Oops. I meant all those things I said to your boss for you. My bad." Ford couldn't believe this had happened to him.

But all those exchanges with her…there had to be something there for him to fall in love *with*.

"What about the funny quotes that would randomly appear on my phone?" He hoped that those were from her. He'd loved getting them. *Please let them be from Gina.*

She looked away. "I sent those."

"Because Monica told you to?"

She shook her head. "My idea."

He looked down at her, into brown eyes that held sadness and something else. Something that gave Ford hope. "One more thing I have to know."

He moved until he stood in her personal space, waiting to see if she moved back. She didn't.

Tilting her chin upward, he kissed her gently, feeling her lips quiver. A whole earthquake was going on inside him. He pulled back an inch, his heart thudding. "I think I'm engaged to the wrong woman. What do you think?"

Gina's arms encircled his neck and she pulled him to her, opening her mouth beneath his. "That's what I think, too."

GINA WAS SHAKING as she unfolded the lounge chair, tossed the robe aside and lay down. She was so fired.

And kissing Ford like that? "He started it" was not a good enough reason. It was wrong and she knew it. He was still her boss's fiancé. Even knowing that, she'd pressed up against him, deepening the kiss when his hands had caressed her bare back. She'd sucked on his tongue, she'd dragged her fingers through his hair, she'd nibbled on his lower lip and she'd shamelessly ground her pelvis against his groin.

So much for hiding her feelings.

When she'd let him go, the man had looked shell-shocked.

And turned on.

Gina closed her eyes. She'd always known she'd get hurt, but she hadn't meant to hurt Ford and Monica, too.

She heard him open the door. That was quick. Gina had no idea what to say to him, or what he'd say to her.

"Want to help me throw calla lilies overboard?"

That was unexpected. Gina sat up. Ford climbed the steps with the calla lilies from the vase below.

"What are you doing?"

"*We* are de-Monica-izing our weekend getaway." He threw a lily overboard. "It's symbolic."

"You and Monica broke up."

"Oh, yes." Ford handed her half the flowers.

"I'm sorry."

"No, you're not. You should have kissed me like that a long time ago. It really clarified things for me."

He thought she'd deliberately set out to sabotage their relationship. Gina didn't know whether it was worth it to explain. It would be easier if she let him blame her. "But I'm sorry you and Monica went through a broken engagement."

"It's our own fault." Ford sat on the lounger next to her. "We had a summer romance that couldn't last when we got back to our real lives. If it hadn't been for you, we would have broken up long before this." He flung another lily into the lake. "You did your job too well. And Monica said to tell you that you aren't fired and that she's hurt you'd even think so."

Gina threw a lily. "Now you're doing what I did. She didn't say that last part."

"Words to that effect."

Gina laughed and threw another calla lily.

Ford dumped the rest of his flowers. "I do have a problem." He leaned back against the lounge chair. "I'm in love with the person who wrote those texts and e-mails and sent me the funny quotes."

A lily dropped to the deck. Ford picked it up and tossed it over the side. "I thought it was Monica. But it's you."

Gina stared at him as she unconsciously crushed the remaining flower stems. He loved her? That *was* what he was saying, right?

When she didn't respond, he gathered the mangled callas from her paralyzed hands and dropped the last of Monica's favorite flower over the side.

"So why is that a problem, you wonder? Because I think you might like me a little."

"I might like you a lot."

His eyes crinkled. "So here's the situation. We're on this wonderfully romantic weekend that I planned for another woman. A woman who I was engaged to not that long ago. Less than ten minutes ago, actually. But now I find I'm here with the woman I love. Which I did not know until I saw her sitting on the bed, also not that long ago."

"Why then?"

"Because I was glad it was you sitting on that bed and not Monica."

"Oh."

"*My* reaction was a little different." He raised his eyebrows and rubbed the space between them.

She smiled and her smile grew the longer she thought about it. "About your problem?"

He drew his knuckles down her cheek. "I don't know the correct amount of time to allow between ending an engagement to one woman and making love to another."

"I don't think there are any strict rules about the time. The ending is the important part."

"See, I think the beginning is the important part. I don't want to come off like an opportunistic jerk. This—" he gestured around them "—was another woman's weekend."

"No." Gina stood and held out her hand. "You planned it for the woman you love. That makes it *my* weekend."

5

TAKING HER HAND, Ford stood and led her toward the pilot-house. "I want to show you this."

They walked along the edge of the boat and then climbed a metal ladder to the top.

"You can access the pilothouse from the back way up here, or the front below." Ford opened a hatch and stepped down, turning to help Gina.

Two club chairs sat in front of the boat's controls. "Directly behind us is an extra sleeping alcove." The bed looked large enough, but the ceiling was only two feet above it. Not exactly the love nest she'd been hoping for.

"Watch." Ford flipped a lever and the ceiling retracted, leaving a clear window above the alcove.

"That's kind of cool."

"Not done yet." He pressed a control somewhere and the window slid open.

"It's a moon roof!" Okay. She saw where he was going with this.

"Climb on up."

Gina did so and stretched out on her back, looking up at the evening sky. How like him to want to be connected to nature while making love.

She heard Ford toe off his deck shoes and when he climbed up, he'd removed his shirt.

He sat with his head and shoulders through the open ceiling. "It's a pretty view. Want to take a look?"

Gina smiled at his naked torso. "I think my line is 'I'm already looking at a pretty view.'"

He grinned down at her, but stayed seated.

Gina got up on her knees and hugged his back. Looking over his shoulder, she saw the green shores of the narrow, twisted lake. She knew there were houses dotting the hills, but they were part of the landscape and not fighting with it.

Ford needed to live in an area like this. If he had to live in the center of a hip, urban area, he wouldn't be Ford anymore.

He ran his hands along her arms. "I don't want to rush you or pressure you into doing something you don't really want to do."

So sensitive and thoughtful.

But there was such a thing as overthinking.

"Ford?" Gina spoke into his ear. "Do you remember the way I kissed you?"

"Best kiss ever."

"You think?" She let go of him and lay back on the bed. "Then you ought to try kissing me when you *aren't* engaged to somebody else."

In an instant, he was beside her, scooping her into his arms and kissing her cheek, her temple, her nose—her nose?—her chin, and finally, when she was about to go crazy, he kissed her mouth. Ah. She settled in, parted her lips and deepened the kiss. She touched her tongue to his. And… And…

She stopped. "Ford?" She traced his lower lip.

"Hmm?" He nuzzled her jaw.

Nuzzled. Nuzzling was nice but this wasn't nuzzling time. This was long-suppressed-physical-desire time. This was an explosion-of-need time. This was Gina-getting-the-chance-she'd-never-thought-she'd-have time.

"Ford."

He drew back.

"This is not the best kiss ever."

Rolling to his back, he drew her to his side. "I don't want to jump you like some sex-crazed maniac. I want you to know my emotions are involved."

"You know, I'd really like to get your penis involved. Do you mind if I jump *you* like a sex-crazed maniac?"

He grinned. "A true sex-crazed maniac wouldn't have asked."

Straddling him, Gina unhooked her bikini top and shimmied out of it. She tossed her head so her hair fell behind her shoulders and let him look at her. For months, his eyes had been friendly, amused, tired, serious. Now, she wanted to see them darken with desire.

And they did.

"So beautiful." His voice was rough.

When he reached to touch her, she intercepted his hand and brought it to her lips. Drawing his index finger into her mouth, she sucked on it, swirling her tongue around and around.

Ford's chest rose and fell.

Gina squirmed against the hard length trapped in the shorts he wore.

"Gina!"

Slowly, she released his finger and used it to rub back and forth across her nipple until it peaked. "Mmm." She squirmed some more.

Ford was breathing through his mouth now, his eyes nearly black. Holding his gaze, Gina drew his finger down her abdomen until it reached the edge of her bikini bottom.

He stopped breathing.

She smiled.

And then she pushed past the edge, through her curls until his finger was nestled against the very best spot. She rubbed her body against it, groaning softly and biting her lower lip. Her excitement built much faster than she'd expected and she had to back off. "Are you sure you don't want to jump me like a sex-crazed maniac?" she asked in a breathy voice.

He twisted his hand from beneath hers and ripped off her bikini bottoms. "I might have been too quick to judge." He flipped her over with gratifying efficiency.

So Mr. Sensitive didn't mean Mr. Wuss. Gina ran her hands over his ribs and as far up his chest as she could reach.

Sitting up on his knees, Ford pulled a condom from a pocket, put it in the palm of one of her wandering hands and got out of his shorts while she opened it.

Moments later, he lay on top of her, kissing her as though he could draw her into him even as he slid into her.

Gina gasped, and then, startling them both, she burst into tears. "I'm n-n-not a crier! I'm a moaner and-d-d occasionally a screamer. I promise."

Ford nuzzled her neck and this time it was the right thing to do. "It's just your emotions. They must be really involved."

"Of course they are! I love you and I had to hide it for so l-long!"

"Shh." He kissed her cheek and licked at a tear.

"It was horrible. What if you'd never—"

"But I did." Ford started thrusting in time with the rocking of the boat.

Gina stopped crying. Funny how that worked.

"Oh, Ford…"

"Nobody here but us sex-crazed maniacs."

She giggled until he lifted her hips and moved faster and deeper.

"Ford!" It was as though they'd gone from the slow lane to the autobahn and were zooming toward the Magical City of O.

Gina clutched at his shoulders. In the background, she heard an outboard-motor boat roar past. Moments later, its wake reached the *Sarah June* and lapped at the hull.

The extra movement set off a throbbing pleasure that rolled

through Gina. She still felt the ripples as Ford tensed and gasped her name.

As they lay, still breathing heavily, limbs entwined, Gina smiled. "That was a nice touch—saying my name like that."

"Mmm?" He traced lazy circles on her shoulder.

"You said, 'Gina.'"

"That's your name."

"I know, but…you could have forgotten and said 'Monica.'"

"No." He nudged her until she was looking at him. "I know exactly who I'm with and exactly who I want to be with. Fortunately, it's the same person. You."

"I don't want to live in a cave."

He blinked. "Sometime, you'll have to tell me how you got from me calling your name in a moment of deepest passion to cave dwelling."

"I want to be sure you know who I am."

Cuddling her, he asked, "Will you look at the mock-up of the house before you call it a cave?"

"Of course."

"Anything else?"

"I'm not a green activist."

"I know. You don't have to be."

"But I will try to be more conscious of our effect on the environment."

"Fair enough."

Gina hesitated. "Is there something I need to know about you?"

"Yes." Ford pulled her on top of him. "I'm really intrigued by the idea of you as a screamer."

Gina laughed. "So give it your best shot, tree hugger."

Later that night, in the middle of a hushed and placid Lake Travis, a woman screamed.

Twice.

Epilogue

"WILLIAM—"

"Tonight we're Beth Ann and Bill," he reminded her. As he had done several times.

The dinner was excellent, the wine was extraordinary and William—Bill—was a witty and amusing companion. A witty and amusing and devastatingly handsome companion.

Not the Bill she remembered.

Except for the good-looking part. She remembered that. It was the devastatingly handsome part that had crept up on her.

The beautifully tailored suit he wore hadn't come from Tuxedo Park's inventory. He looked better, more successful and sophisticated. Julian Wainright himself had come by their table and greeted Bill as a friend. Julian defined Beth Ann's idea of sophistication, and tonight, Bill was his peer.

And the way he'd focused intently on her all evening had her running hot and cold.

He found her attractive and he was making sure she knew it. That made her hot. Wondering what to do about it made her cold.

He appeared casually relaxed, content to wait for…she wished she knew. Or was it she was afraid she knew?

She shouldn't have let Lia talk her into wearing this jacket. It sent the wrong signal.

"We should probably discuss the men's vests," she said.

Bill set his wineglass down. "We should not."

"Then what should we discuss?"

"How about we talk about me waiting the last eight years for you?"

Beth Ann was afraid she was going to cough up her sea bass because of the sudden knot in her throat.

"I could tell that the timing was never right, but damn, woman, you're worth the wait."

Beth Ann choked down her food. "I never led you on. I never implied we were anything more than business partners."

"But you knew how I felt." He gazed steadily at her.

Beth Ann felt her cheeks heat and went for her water glass.

"I was happy at the Monkey Suit, but I sold up and followed you here to Rocky Falls because this is what you wanted."

"You didn't have to." She should have seen this coming. He was right—she had guessed that he felt something for her.

"If I wanted to be with you, I did."

"Don't pretend that this hasn't been a great partnership and that you haven't benefited from my ideas."

"Never said it wasn't."

"I've worked *hard*—"

"Never said you hadn't. And you just landed a wedding big enough to take you to the next level."

"To take *us* to the next level."

Bill picked up his wine and studied the liquid through the candlelight. "I don't know if I want to go there with you or get out while the gettin's good."

She felt frozen. "What are you saying?"

He set the glass back down. Reaching across the table, he covered one of her cold hands with his. "I'm saying that I've been in love with you since your bad-perm days. One look at you all excited about opening your first shop and I fell so hard and so fast, I woke up in a different world. Since I met you, you're my last thought at night and my first thought in the morning. Every. Single. Day." His eyes were as intense as she'd ever seen them.

"Bill," she whispered.

He squeezed her hand and withdrew his. "I've been waiting for the right time for you, and today I decided that it was the right time for me."

Beth Ann was sweating in the sample jacket. "What do you want me to say?"

Hurt and disappointment flashed briefly across his face. "I want to know if you can ever feel that way about me."

Beth Ann's heart was pounding so hard she could barely breathe. She wasn't ready to think about this. She couldn't think about this. There was too much going on. With the exposure from the Brantley wedding, she was going to be busier than ever. He was putting pressure on her. She—

Her cell phone rang.

"Don't answer," Bill said quietly.

Beth Ann was already looking at the number. "It's Lia."

"Beth Ann. Call her back in a few minutes."

"It's…it's got to be an emergency. She wouldn't call me otherwise." Beth Ann jabbed at the talk button. "Lia?"

She turned away with her finger in her other ear even though she could hear perfectly well. But she didn't want to look at Bill.

It was bad enough meeting his eyes when she disconnected. "The computer crashed and Lia lost all the orders including the Brantleys'." Beth Ann gathered her purse and stood.

"Sit."

"Didn't you hear what I said? This is a disaster."

Bill drank his wine.

"We need to leave."

"Finish your dinner. The computer is going to stay crashed whether you eat or not, and there's nothing you can do until tomorrow."

"I can help re-create the orders."

"You can do that tomorrow."

"Bill!"

He set the empty glass down with such force, the stem snapped. Staring at it, he took a deep breath. "Here." He reached into his pocket and tossed his keys onto the table. "Take my truck."

"But…"

"I'm staying here tonight. In the Rocky Falls Suite. Send James or somebody to pick me up tomorrow."

"You…you reserved the Rocky Falls Suite? The one with the two-story waterfall?"

He said nothing, his face stony.

As though it was happening to somebody else, Beth Ann saw her hand reach for the ring of keys. "I'm sorry," she whispered.

Dazed, she drove his truck to the salon.

She listened to what Lia was saying, but it was Bill and the expression on his face when she'd taken the keys that dominated her thoughts.

She heard enough to know that what had happened was bad, but it wasn't a disaster like having the building catch fire.

The elegant salon was her dream. William—Bill's partnership had given her that dream. His jokes and casual ways had balanced her pretentions. Had kept her focused. Kept her sane.

And now he was going to leave. Knowing Bill, he'd walk away and let her have everything.

Right at that moment, Beth Ann knew she didn't want the bridal salon without Bill.

She blinked as Lia said something about the Brantley pinks. "It'll be fine," she told her vaguely. "Just finish up here and go on home."

Beth Ann didn't remember the details of the drive back to the Wainright in Bill's truck. She remembered shaking with nerves. She remembered the elevator ride to the top floor and desperately trying to think of what she was going to say.

She remembered walking down the hall to the end opposite the bridal suite, where she'd delivered so many dresses.

And now she stood at the door with her hand poised to knock and noticed that there was a doorbell. That made sense. The famed Rocky Falls Suite with its outdoor balcony and hot tub that replicated the falls needed a doorbell because discreet knocks wouldn't be heard outside.

Beth Ann knocked anyway. And she rang the bell, too. And then she rang it again.

It seemed as though an eternity passed before Bill opened the door. He barely wore a casually knotted terry robe. His chest and hair were wet. His face was blank.

"Did monsieur ring for zee French maid?"

He just stared at her and Beth Ann was terrified that she was too late.

"That is the worst French accent I've ever heard. Get in here." He pulled her into the suite and into his arms and into a kiss that threatened to devour her.

Desire, passion and pure lust bloomed within her. Why had she been afraid? She slipped her hands beneath his robe as his fingers quickly unbuttoned the lace jacket.

A benefit of being in their profession was that they were experts in dressing and undressing. Beth Ann shucked her skirt and heard Bill inhale sharply.

"Beth Ann Grakowski, where are your panties?" Bill seemed genuinely shocked and not teasing at all.

What was the matter with him? "I'm wearing panty hose." Probably the last woman on earth to do so. She rolled them over her hips.

Bill seemed to be breathing hard. Maybe he was a stocking man. Good to know.

"Y-you mean to tell me that all those years I gave you foot rubs, you weren't wearing any panties?"

"Panty. Hose." She finished pulling them off.

Bill took them and held them up. "See. Through."

"So? No one is going to be looking."

He made a strangled sound, scooped her up in his arms and carried her out to the patio. Without pausing, he descended into the lush pool, designed to look like a forest grotto and waterfall. "Beth Ann, from now on, your foot rubs are going to be a little different."

* * * * *

Celebrate 60 years of pure reading
pleasure with Harlequin®!

Harlequin Presents® is proud to
introduce its gripping new miniseries,
THE ROYAL HOUSE OF KAREDES.
An exquisite coronation diamond,
split as a symbol of a warring royal family's
feud, is missing! But whoever reunites
the diamond halves will rule all....

Welcome to eight brand-new titles that unfold to
reveal the stories of kings and queens, princes
and princesses torn apart by pride and power,
but finally reunited by love.

Step into the world of Karedes with
BILLIONAIRE PRINCE, PREGNANT MISTRESS
Available July 2009
from Harlequin Presents®.

ALEXANDROS KAREDES, SNOW dusting the shoulders of his leather jacket and glittering like jewels in his dark hair, stood at the door. Maria felt the blood drain from her head.

"Good evening, Ms. Santos."

His voice was as she remembered it. Deep. Husky. Perfect English, but with the faintest hint of a Greek accent. And cold, as cold as it had been that awful morning she would never forget, when he'd accused her of horrible things, called her terrible names....

"Aren't you going to ask me in?"

She fought for composure. Last time they'd faced each other, they'd been on his turf. Now they were on hers. She was in command here, and that meant everything.

"There's a sign on the door downstairs," she said, her tone every bit as frigid as his. "It says, 'No soliciting or vagrants.'"

His lips drew back in a wolfish grin. "Very amusing."

"What do you want, Prince Alexandros?"

A tight smile eased across his mouth and it killed her that even now, knowing he was a vicious, arrogant man, she couldn't help but notice what a handsome mouth it was. Chiseled. Generous. Beautiful, like the rest of him, which made him living proof that beauty could, indeed, be only skin deep.

"Such formality, Maria. You were hardly so proper the last time we were together."

She knew his choice of words was deliberate. She felt her face heat; she couldn't help that but she damned well didn't have to let him lure her into a verbal sparring match.

"I'll ask you once more, your highness. What do you want?"

"Ask me in and I'll tell you."

"I have no intention of asking you in. Tell me why you're here or don't. It's your choice, just as it will be my choice to shut the door in your face."

He laughed. It infuriated her but she could hardly blame him. He was tall—six-two, six-three—and though he stood with one shoulder leaning against the door frame, hands tucked casually into the pockets of the jacket, his pose was deceptive. He was strong, with the leanly muscled body of a well-trained athlete.

She remembered his body with painful clarity. The feel of him under her hands. The power of him moving over her. The taste of him on her tongue.

Suddenly, he straightened, his laughter gone. "I have not come this distance to stand in your doorway," he said coldly, "and I am not going to leave until I am ready to do so. I suggest you stand aside and stop behaving like a petulant child."

A petulant child? Was that what he thought? This man who had spent hours making love to her and had then accused her of—of trading her body for profit?

Except it had not been love, it had been sex. And the sooner she got rid of him, the better.

She let go of the doorknob and stepped aside. "You have five minutes."

He strolled past her, bringing cold air and the scent of the night with him. She swung toward him, arms folded. He reached past her, pushed the door closed, then folded his arms, too. She wanted to open the door again but she'd be damned if she was going to get into a who's-in-charge-here argument with him. She was in charge, and he would surely see a tussle over the ground rules as a sign of weakness.

Instead, she looked past him at the big clock above her work table.

"Ten seconds gone," she said briskly. "You're wasting time, your highness."

"What I have to say will take longer than five minutes."

"Then you'll just have to learn to economize. More than five minutes, I'll call the police."

Instantly, his hand was wrapped around her wrist. He tugged her toward him, his dark chocolate eyes almost black with anger.

"You do that and I'll tell every tabloid shark I can contact about how Maria Santos tried to buy a five-hundred-thousand-dollar commission by seducing a prince." He smiled thinly. "They'll lap it up."

* * * * *

What will it take for this billionaire prince to realize he's falling in love with his mistress…?
Look for
BILLIONAIRE PRINCE, PREGNANT MISTRESS
by Sandra Marton
Available July 2009 from Harlequin Presents®.

We'll be spotlighting a different series every month throughout 2009 to celebrate our 60th anniversary.

Look for Harlequin® Presents in July!

THE ROYAL HOUSE *of* KAREDES

TWO CROWNS, TWO ISLANDS, ONE LEGACY
A royal family, torn apart by pride and its lust for power, reunited by purity and passion

Step into the world of Karedes beginning this July with

BILLIONAIRE PRINCE, PREGNANT MISTRESS
by
Sandra Marton

Eight volumes to collect and treasure!

REQUEST YOUR FREE BOOKS!

2 FREE NOVELS PLUS 2 FREE GIFTS!

HARLEQUIN®

Blaze™

Red-hot reads!

YES! Please send me 2 FREE Harlequin® Blaze™ novels and my 2 FREE gifts (gifts are worth about $10). After receiving them, if I don't wish to receive any more books, I can return the shipping statement marked "cancel". If I don't cancel, I will receive 6 brand-new novels every month and be billed just $4.24 per book in the U.S. or $4.71 per book in Canada. That's a savings of 15% off the cover price. It's quite a bargain. Shipping and handling is just 50¢ per book.* I understand that accepting the 2 free books and gifts places me under no obligation to buy anything. I can always return a shipment and cancel at any time. Even if I never buy another book, the two free books and gifts are mine to keep forever.

151 HDN EYS2 351 HDN EYTE

Name	(PLEASE PRINT)	
Address		Apt. #
City	State/Prov.	Zip/Postal Code

Signature (if under 18, a parent or guardian must sign)

Mail to the **Harlequin Reader Service:**

IN U.S.A.: P.O. Box 1867, Buffalo, NY 14240-1867
IN CANADA: P.O. Box 609, Fort Erie, Ontario L2A 5X3

Not valid to current subscribers of Harlequin Blaze books.

Want to try two free books from another line?
Call 1-800-873-8635 or visit www.morefreebooks.com.

* Terms and prices subject to change without notice. Prices do not include applicable taxes. N.Y. residents add applicable sales tax. Canadian residents will be charged applicable provincial taxes and GST. Offer not valid in Quebec. This offer is limited to one order per household. All orders subject to approval. Credit or debit balances in a customer's account(s) may be offset by any other outstanding balance owed by or to the customer. Please allow 4 to 6 weeks for delivery. Offer available while quantities last.

Your Privacy: Harlequin Books is committed to protecting your privacy. Our Privacy Policy is available online at www.eHarlequin.com or upon request from the Reader Service. From time to time we make our lists of customers available to reputable third parties who may have a product or service of interest to you. If you would prefer we not share your name and address, please check here. ☐

HB09R3

 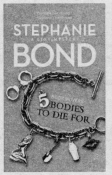 

In 2009 Harlequin celebrates
60 years of pure reading pleasure!

We're marking this occasion by offering
16 **FREE** full books to download and read.

Visit

www.HarlequinCelebrates.com

to choose from a variety of
great romance stories
that are absolutely **FREE!**

(Total approximate retail value of $60)

We invite you to visit and share the Web site
with your friends, family
and anyone who enjoys reading.

You're invited to join our Tell Harlequin Reader Panel!

By joining our new reader panel you will:

- Receive Harlequin® books—they are FREE and yours to keep with no obligation to purchase anything!
- Participate in fun online surveys
- Exchange opinions and ideas with women just like you
- Have a say in our new book ideas and help us publish the best in women's fiction

In addition, you will have a chance to win great prizes and receive special gifts! See Web site for details. Some conditions apply. Space is limited.

To join, visit us at

www.TellHarlequin.com.

HARLEQUIN® *Blaze*™

COMING NEXT MONTH
Available June 30, 2009

#477 ENDLESS SUMMER Julie Kenner, Karen Anders, Jill Monroe
Three surfer chicks + three hot guys = one endless summer. The Maui beaches will never be the same after these couples hit the waves and live their sexiest dreams to the fullest!

#478 HARD TO RESIST Samantha Hunter
American Heroes
Sexy, straight-as-an-arrow Texas Ranger Jarod Wyatt is awestruck by the New York skyline and the stunning photographer snapping his portrait. As soon as Lacey Graham spies the hunk through her lens she knows she has to have him…even if she has to commit a crime to get the good cop's attention!

#479 MAKE ME YOURS Betina Krahn
Blaze Historicals
Mariah Eller was only trying to save her inn from being trashed. So how did she manage to attract the unwanted—and erotic—attention of the Prince of Wales? Not that being desired by royalty is bad—except Mariah much prefers Jack St. Lawrence, the prince's sexy best friend….

#480 TWIN SEDUCTION Cara Summers
The Wrong Bed: Again and Again
Jordan Ware is in over her head. According to her late mother's will, she is to trade places with a twin sister she didn't know she had. She thinks it will be tricky, but possible…until she finds herself in bed with her twin's fiancé.

#481 THE SOLDIER Rhonda Nelson
Uniformly Hot!
Army Ranger Adam McPherson is back home, thanks to a roadside bomb that cost him part of his leg. But he's not out yet. He's been offered a position in the Special Forces once he's back on his feet. The problem? His childhood nemesis seems determined to keep him off his feet—and in her bed….

#482 THE MIGHTY QUINNS: TEAGUE Kate Hoffmann
Quinns Down Under
Romeo and Juliet, Outback-style. Teague Quinn has loved Haley Fraser since they were both kids. But time and feuding families got in the way. Now Teague and Haley are both back home—and back in bed! Can they make first love last the second time around?

HBCNMBPA0609